Mulvihill, Margaret.
The treasury of saints and
martyrs /
CC 1065000240 FEB   2005

THE TREASURY
OF
SAINTS
AND MARTYRS

Margaret Mulvihill

Consultant: David Hugh Farmer

Viking

Picture Acknowledgments

Front Cover e.t.archive; Back Cover (top) A.K.G. London. (bottom) Ashmolean Museum/Bridgeman Art Library.

l = left; r = right; b = bottom; t = top; c = center

1 (title page) SCALA; 2 e.t.archive; 3 A.K.G.; 4 e.t.archive; 5tr Pinacoteca Civica, Fermo/Bridgeman Art Library; 6t York City Art Gallery/Bridgeman Art Library; 6b Museo Episcopal de Vic, Catalonia/Bridgeman Art Library; 7tr & bl A.K.G.; 8tl A.K.G.; 8br e.t.archive; 9 A.K.G.; 10bl A.K.G.; 11 A.K.G.; 12-14 A.K.G.; 15 e.t.archive; 16tr Mary Evans Picture Library; 16bl Prado Madrid/Index/Bridgeman Art Library; 16 br Sonia Halliday Photographs; 17t Santa Maria de Popolo, Rome/Bridgeman Art Library; 18 e.t.archive; 19tr Louvre, Paris/Peter Willi/Bridgeman Art Library; 19bl A.K.G.; 20r Phillips, The Fine Art Aucioneers/Bridgeman Art Library; 21 A.K.G.; 22bl A.K.G.; 22br Sonia Halliday Photographs; 23t A.K.G.; 24 e.t.archive; 25tr e.t.archive; 26 Fitzwilliam Museum, University of Cambridge/Bridgeman Art Library; 27tr e.t.archive; 27bl SCALA; 28 Agnew & Sons, London/Bridgeman Art Library; 29tr SCALA; 29bl Robert Harding Picture Library; 30l e.t.archive; 31 Johnny van Haeften Gallery, London; 32tl Sonia Halliday Photographs; 33 e.t.archive; 34t Ashmolean Museum, Oxford/Bridgeman Art Library; 34br Duomo, Florence/Bridgeman Art Library; 35 Sonia Halliday Photographs; 36r National Gallery, London/Corbis; 37l e.t.archive; 38tl Huntington Library & Art Gallery, USA/Bridgeman Art Library; 39r The Hutchison Library/P.W.Rippon; 40t e.t.archive; 41t e.t.archive; 42 Sonia Halliday Photographs; 43r Nationalgalerie, Berlin/Bildarchiv Steffens/Bridgeman Art Library; 44t Robert Harding Picture Library; 45 Roudnice Lobkowicz Collection, Nelahozeves Castle, Czech Republic/Bridgeman Art Library; 46 Mary Evans Picture Library; 47t Hospital de la Santa Caridad, Seville/Giraudon/Bridgeman Art Library; 48t British Library, London/Bridgeman Art Library; 49tr Kurpfalzisches Museum, Heidelberg/ Giraudon/Bridgeman Art Library; 49bl Frick Collection, New York/Bridgeman Art Library; 50t Galleria degli Uffizi, Florence/Bridgeman Art Library; 51tr & bl A.K.G.; 52t & bl A.K.G.; 52tr Palazzo Ducale, Urbino/Bridgeman Art Library; 53tl The Stock Market; 53tr e.t.archive; 54l Tony Stone Images/Joe Cornish; 55t Santa Trinita, Florence/Bridgeman Art Library; 55bl Monasterio de El Escorial, Spain/ Bridgeman Art Library; 55br Mary Evans Picture Library; 56t e.t.archive; 57t e.t.archive; 58l Abegg-Stiftung, Riggisberg/ Bridgeman Art Library; 59t Museo de Bellas Artes, Seville/Bridgeman Art Library; 60br Statens Historiska Museum/Gunnel Jansson; 61tl A.K.G.; 61r Vadstena Turistbyra; 62 A.K.G.; 63l A.K.G.; 64l Musee de Sibiu, Romania/Giraudon/Bridgeman Art Library; 65 Chateau de Versailles/ Giraudon/Bridgeman Art Library; 66l Private Collection/Index/Bridgeman Art Library; 66r SCALA; 67l SCALA; 67r The Hutchison Library/ John Hatt; 68l Sonia Halliday Photographs; 69 Museo Lazara Galdiano, Madrid/Bridgeman Art Library; 70r The Hutchison Library/Juliet Highet; 71r Palazzo Pitti, Florence/Bridgeman Art Library; 72b Musee de l'Assistance Publique, Hospitaux de Paris/Giraudon/Bridgeman Art Library; 73 Musee de l'Assistance Publique, Hospitaux de Paris/Giraudon/Bridgeman Art Library; 74l Courtesy, St Joseph's Provincial House Archives; 75r Courtesy, St.Joseph's Provincial House Archives; 76c A.K.G.; 76br The Hutchison Library/Sarah Errington; 77t Courtesy, Archivio L.D.C.; 77b Courtesy, Mount Saint Bernard Abbey.

All other illustrations courtesy of Dover Publications.

VIKING
Published by the Penguin Group
Penguin Putnam Books for Young Readers,
345 Hudson Street,
New York, New York 10014, USA

Penguin Books Ltd, Registered Offices:
Harmondsworth, Middlesex, England

First published in the UK by Marshall
Publishing Ltd, 1999

First published in the United States of
America by Viking, a division of Penguin
Putnam Books for Young Readers, 1999

Copyright © Marshall Editions Ltd, 1999

All rights reserved

ISBN 0-670-88789-7

Library of Congress Catalog Card Number:
99-70893

Printed in Singapore.

A 15th-century Italian fresco of Saint Benedict and his monks.

CONTENTS

Saint Paul painted
by the French
artist Poussin
(1594–1665).

WHAT IS A SAINT?

THE WORD "SAINT" comes from the Latin *sanctus*, which means sacred. The saints of Christian tradition are exceptional men and women who managed to come close to God in their own lifetimes. For nearly 2,000 years they have been celebrated as the heroes of Christianity.

Every saint has a story, and there is a story and a saint for every human circumstance. Over centuries the ranks of the saints have been swelled by people of all ages and both sexes and from all walks of life. Martin of Tours, a Roman officer's son, was 80 when he died; 1,000 years later, Joan of Arc, the daughter of peasants, was 19 when she was burned at the stake. The cults of 10,000 saints have been identified by church historians, and thousands more have been forgotten. Not surprisingly, the most popular saints have the most memorable stories. In some cases the story has been so embroidered over time that the real person who may have inspired it is quite lost. Saint Christopher, for example, is hard to locate in a historical time and place. Saint Patrick, by contrast, wrote the story of his life when he was an old man. He wanted to show that he was an ordinary person who did not deserve to be regarded as a saint, but his *Confession* reveals him as a brave and honest man who, against many odds, established Christianity among the pagan Irish.

In the days when few people could read, the stories or legends of the saints were read

The saints are admired for their good deeds. Here Saint Lucy, a fourth-century martyr, hands out food to the poor.

aloud on their feast days, the days on which they had died or been martyred. Particular saints were adopted as patrons by professions or places they had some special connection to.

According to the Catholic Church, the dead saints are with God in heaven. For the Orthodox Church, saints are "sleeping" like the rest of the dead, but they can expect eternal life after the Day of Judgment. Both churches encourage devotion to the saints, the friends of God, to whom the faithful can appeal for spiritual help and for miracles. Their bodily remains, or relics, are treasured, and they are, with Jesus and Mary, a major source of inspiration for sculptors, painters, and icon-makers. After the Reformation in the 16th century, Christianity was divided in its attitude to the saints, but for all Christians they continue to be regarded as inspiring examples of godly living.

Saint Antony of Padua was a Franciscan friar and priest. He is often prayed to as the finder of lost articles. This painting is by El Greco.

THE MAKING OF SAINTS

Saint Clement of Rome was one of the early popes. He was martyred at sea around the year 100.

THE FIRST SAINTS were the first Christians: the apostles, the evangelists, the Virgin Mary, and the early martyrs. The people who had witnessed a martyr's death knew what he or she had suffered rather than deny Christ, and were sure that everlasting life in heaven was the martyr's "crown," or reward. Christians believed that saints continued to be present in a special way through their relics, or remains. They gathered at the tombs of the martyrs for communion meals and founded churches on their treasured relics.

After the martyrs came the confessors, who confessed their

Christianity at great personal risk, but did not actually die for their faith. As Christianity became the faith of the majority of people in the Roman world, new kinds of heroes were recognized as saints, people who denied themselves every physical comfort so as to be closer to God, or learned teachers. Gradually, the saints came to include bishops, monks, and visionaries as well as martyrs.

This is a detail from a 12th-century altarpiece showing the martyrdom of Saint Margaret of Antioch.

In the early centuries it was enough, if people wished to honor the life and death of a saintly person, for the local bishop to add the new saint's feast day to the Church's calendar. Then, late in the 12th century, Pope Alexander III decided that in the future saints must be canonized, or listed in the Church's calendar, by the authorities in Rome. From then on, saints were made after a detailed inquiry into their lives and works. Once past the first stage, a saintly candidate would be declared *Beatus*, or Blessed. To be declared a saint, he or she had to be shown to have led an especially virtuous life and to have performed a certain number of miracles, which were proof that the dead person was favored by God.

By the 13th century, people such as Thomas Aquinas (*above*) were canonized for their attention to Christian doctrine.

Canonization affected the rise of shrines and pilgrimages in medieval Europe. The enshrined relics of an officially canonized saint attracted huge numbers of pilgrims. The new rules also affected the number and type of people who were canonized. An eighth-century Irish catalog of

Michael the Archangel is honored with the saints for his position as "captain of the heavenly hosts."

saints lists 750 individuals, most of whom were venerated in the localities where they had lived, but after the 12th century it became difficult for a community far from Rome to persuade the Church to canonize a local saint. The most complete record of saints, the 12 volumes of the *Bibliotheca Sanctorum*, lists more than 10,000 saints, but only about 400 of them were canonized by popes after the new rules. The Feast of All Saints on November 1 celebrates all people whose saintliness has gone unrecognized by anyone but God.

THE EARLY DAYS

Christians believe that Jesus died and rose again three days later to bring everlasting salvation to those who follow him.

THE ONLY detailed information we have about Jesus comes from the gospels, which were written by his followers. We know that he was a Jew and that his disciples believed he was Christ, the great leader whose coming had been prophesied in the Old Testament. After three years of preaching, in around the year 30, Jesus was crucified. Fifty days after his Resurrection, on Pentecost, his followers were visited by the Holy Spirit, sent to encourage and comfort them. From then on, they spread the Word that Jesus Christ was the son of God. He had been crucified and raised from the dead, and through him eternal salvation was promised to all.

Christianity did not separate from its beginnings as a movement within Judaism until Saint Paul took the Word to the rest of the Roman Empire. The early Christians eagerly awaited the Second Coming of Jesus Christ, which many believed would happen within their own lifetimes. Their faith sustained them against prejudice and through periods of persecution. Pagan observers were amazed by the willingness of Christians to die for their faith, and they noticed how they shared their food and belongings, and the care that they took of the needy. Christians treated others like their relations, as if they all belonged to one family. "There is no such thing as Jew and Greek, slave and freeman, male and female," Saint Paul told them, "for you are all one in Jesus Christ."

The early Christians regarded all baptized believers as saints. Paul's letter to the Christians of Philippi in Macedonia starts, "Paul and Timothy, the servants of Jesus Christ, to all the saints in Christ Jesus that are in Philippi." Many of these pioneering Christians did also become saints according to later meanings of the word. Peter and Paul were hailed as saints not only because they were leaders of the Church but also because they were martyred. For the first 300 years, saints and martyrs were one and the same thing. But over time, the title of saint became reserved for people who had lived outstandingly holy lives.

Saint Paul (*right*) called all Christians saints.

(*Far right*) The Holy Spirit visits Mary and the apostles at Pentecost.

MARY AND JOSEPH

"Hail Mary, full of grace the Lord is with thee. Blessed art thou among women and blessed is the fruit of thy womb, Jesus. Holy Mary, Mother of God, pray for us sinners now and at the hour of our death. Amen."

The angel Gabriel appeared to Mary to tell her that she was to bear a son. The dove flying down the shaft of light symbolizes the Holy Spirit.

THE BEST LOVED SAINT is Mary, the Mother of God. Her parents were Joachim and Anne, and when she was a baby they presented her at the temple (synagogue) in Jerusalem. As a young, unmarried woman she was visited by the angel Gabriel, who told her that by the power of the Holy Spirit she would bear a son called Jesus. At first Mary was afraid, but then, with amazing calmness, she answered Gabriel, "Behold the handmaid of the Lord! Be it unto me according to thy word." She went to stay with her cousin Elizabeth, who was also expecting a special baby, John the Baptist. Elizabeth welcomed Mary with the words of the Ave Maria (Hail Mary) prayer, "Blessed art thou among women and blessed is the fruit of thy womb." Then Mary said her Magnificat, a song of thanksgiving.

Mary married Joseph, whom the gospels describe as a carpenter and an upright man. He was descended from the royal family of King David and is not likely to have been that much older than his wife, even though artists have tended to depict him as an old man. Joseph took good care of Mary, having been reassured by an angel that she had been made pregnant by the power of the Holy Spirit. After the birth of Jesus in Bethlehem, another angel told Joseph to take his family to Egypt, where they would be safe from the violence of King Herod, who feared the baby boy as a rival for his throne. Joseph is not mentioned again in the gospels until, as he and Mary were making their way back to Nazareth after attending the festival of Passover in Jerusalem, they lost Jesus. Since Jesus was about 12 then, old enough to be

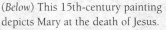

The birth of Jesus is known as the Nativity. This nativity scene was cut into a piece of wood and then painted. It was made in the 15th century in Germany.

(*Below*) This 15th-century painting depicts Mary at the death of Jesus.

with the men in the temple, Mary had thought that he was with Joseph, and Joseph had thought that he was with the other boys. Sick with worry, they rushed back to Jerusalem, where they found him with the rabbis in the temple, listening to them and asking and answering questions. "Don't you know that I had to be about my Father's business?" he asked them.

When Jesus was grown up, Mary stayed in the background, but when they were at the wedding in Cana, she asked him to perform his first miracle, turning the water into wine. She was present at the Crucifixion, where her dying son asked his disciple John to take care of her. By then, Mary must have been a widow. She was with the disciples in Jerusalem in the days before Pentecost, and received the Holy Spirit. There is no further mention of Mary in the gospels, but according to one tradition she spent her last days with John in Ephesus, where she died and was "assumed" straight into heaven.

All over the world Mary is revered as the Madonna, the Blessed Virgin, Our Lady, the Queen of Heaven, the kindest saint.

SAINT JOSEPH IS THE PATRON SAINT OF CARPENTERS, FATHERS, THE FAMILY, THE DYING, SOCIAL JUSTICE, MEXICO, CANADA, AND AUSTRIA.

JOHN THE BAPTIST

DIED C.28–30

(*Above*) Elizabeth and Mary greet each other. They were both pregnant, Elizabeth with John and Mary with Jesus. Elizabeth told Mary that the child in her womb leapt for joy when she saw Mary.

(*Right*) John baptized Jesus in the waters of the River Jordan.

"I baptize you with water for repentance. But after me will come one who is more powerful than I, whose sandals I am not fit to carry. He will baptize you with the Holy Spirit and with fire."

JOHN THE BAPTIST was the son of a priest, Zachary, and his wife Elizabeth, who was related to Mary. Elizabeth and Zachary were an elderly, childless couple when an angel foretold the birth of their son, who was destined to prepare the way for the coming of Christ. When he grew up, John moved away from Jerusalem. He dressed in rough clothes made of camel's hair, lived on locusts and wild honey, and described himself as "the voice of one crying in the wilderness." He became a wandering preacher, moving about the valley of the river Jordan, persuading people to get ready for the Lord whose coming had been prophesied in the Old Testament: "Prepare the way of the Lord, make his paths straight!"

When people came to John and promised to make a fresh start, he baptized them in the waters of the Jordan as a sign that their sins had been washed away. Before they were Jesus' disciples, Peter and Andrew were baptized by John, and then, one day, Jesus himself came down to the river. At first John protested that Jesus did not need to be baptized because he was already without sin, but Jesus insisted. Then John saluted him as "the Lamb of God who takes away the sins of the world." Ever since, baptism has been the rite of entry to the Christian faith.

Soon after he had baptized Jesus, John was hauled into prison for criticizing the local ruler, Herod Antipas. John was protesting the fact that Herod had divorced his first wife in order to marry his half brother's wife, Herodias. Herodias had a daughter called Salome. At Herod's birthday feast, Salome danced for her new stepfather. Herod offered

JOHN THE BAPTIST IS THE PATRON SAINT OF HIGHWAYS, TAILORS, FURRIERS, AND BIRD DEALERS.

to reward her with anything she cared to ask for, so, prompted by her mother, she asked for the head of the troublemaker called John the Baptist. Immediately, an executioner was sent to John's prison, and Salome was presented with his head on a dish. This gruesome scene has inspired many paintings.

John the Baptist is regarded as one of the prophets of Islam and is mentioned in the Koran. He lived and preached in the manner of an Old Testament prophet, and he may have been connected with a group of Jewish holy men who lived in the rocky Qumran region of ancient Palestine. In 1947 an Arab shepherd came across jars containing ancient scrolls of the Qumran community. These texts, the Dead Sea scrolls, stress the need for people to give up their bad habits so that they would be ready for the coming of the Messiah.

PETER AND ANDREW

DIED C. 64   DIED C. 60

(*Below*) A Russian painting of Saint Peter showing him with a key, which is his emblem.

(*Below right*) El Greco's painting of Saint Andrew shows him with the X-shaped cross he is said to have been crucified on.

PETER FIRST APPEARS in the gospels as Simon, the brother of Andrew. They were fishermen from Galilee. Simon was married, and Andrew lived with him and his wife and mother-in-law in a house at Capernaum. They had their own boat and worked as a fishing team with another pair of brothers, James and John. Before they became disciples of Jesus, Simon and Andrew had been baptized by John the Baptist. Andrew introduced his brother to Jesus, who singled him out as the leader of the apostles by giving him a new name, Cephas, meaning rock, which is *petros* in Greek.

After the miraculous catch, when there were so many fish that the nets nearly broke, Peter went everywhere with Jesus. Jesus cured his mother-in-law of a fever, and Peter was there when Jesus brought the daughter of Jairus back to life. Peter saw Jesus walking upon the waters and nearly drowned trying to imitate him. He was there at the Transfiguration, when Jesus talked with the prophets Elias and Moses. Peter did not always understand Jesus' teachings immediately, and he asked a lot of questions. Although he never wavered in his rock-like faith, he found it hard to control his temper. He fell asleep in the Garden of Gethsemane, and it was to him that Jesus said, "the spirit is willing but the flesh is weak." When Jesus was arrested, Peter drew a sword and attacked one of the guards. However, later, when he was in the courtyard of Pontius Pilate's house and someone asked him if he was a friend of Jesus, he was too scared to say yes.

(*Left*) When Peter was waiting outside the court where Jesus was being tried, he was asked if he knew Jesus. Peter denied it three times. This painting depicts one of Peter's denials, to a palace maid who is asking if he is one of Jesus' followers.

Peter never forgave himself for his moments of weakness, even though Jesus did, but after the Crucifixion he was the undisputed leader of the Christians of Jerusalem. At first, he was not as sure as Paul that the Christian message should be taken to the wider world of the Gentiles rather than just to the Jews. But once he had made up his mind, Peter was a rock. Around the year 43 he was imprisoned by Herod Agrippa, but he escaped and made his way to Rome, where he is said to have spent the last 20 years of his life. When Emperor Nero began persecuting Christians in Rome, Peter's friends begged him to go into hiding. As he hurried away from the city, Jesus appeared to him. Ashamed for leaving his flock, he hurried back to certain death. He asked to be crucified upside down, as he did not think he was worthy to die in the same position as Jesus.

Less is known of Andrew's life after the death of Jesus. It is said that he went to preach in the area around the Black Sea and was martyred at Patras in Greece, on an X-shaped cross. His relics were taken to Byzantium 300 years later, which, as Constantinople, was the new capital of the Eastern Roman Empire. Andrew has a special place in the history of the Orthodox Church. He is also patron saint of Scotland, where his cross is the national emblem.

SAINT ANDREW IS THE PATRON SAINT OF RUSSIA, GREECE, SCOTLAND, FISHERMEN, AND SPINSTERS.

SAINT PETER IS THE PATRON SAINT OF ROME, POPES, FISHERMEN, AND BUTCHERS.

PAUL

DIED C.67

PAUL came from a wealthy family in Tarsus. By trade, he was a tent maker, but he knew how to speak and write Greek and he had been educated in Jewish law by a leading Jerusalem rabbi. Originally, he thought the Christians should be persecuted for spreading a mistaken version of the Jewish religion. He even watched the stoning of the first martyr, Stephen.

Paul was on his way to the city of Damascus when he had the experience that changed his life. A sudden bolt of light from the sky caused him to fall from his horse. As he lay on the ground, he heard Jesus rebuking him for his campaign against the Christians, and telling him that he was destined to bring the Word to the Gentiles. Paul decided to be baptized, and around the year 45, he set out on the first of his three great missionary journeys, which would take him to Cyprus and through Asia Minor, Syria, Macedonia, and Greece. When he moved on, he kept in touch by letter with the communities which he had helped to establish. These letters, the *Epistles*, are part of the New Testament.

Many of Jerusalem's Jews resented Paul's missions for much the same reasons as he had first resented the

An image of Paul painted by Velázquez in 1619.

Paul was invited to speak to Greek philosophers at the Propylaea in Athens. Only a few were convinced by his message.

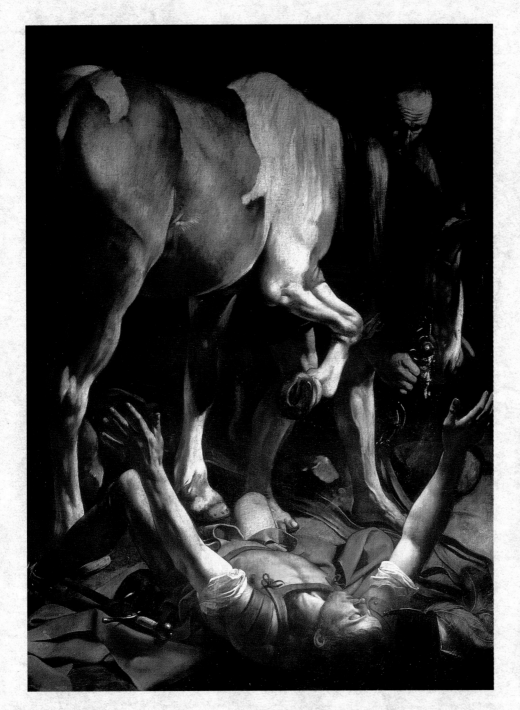

A dramatic painting of Paul's vision on the way to Damascus. The artist, Caravaggio, has created a scene which symbolizes the moment. In the darkness a light shines out to Paul, throwing him from his horse with its power.

SAINT PAUL IS
THE PATRON SAINT OF
TENT MAKERS, WEAVERS,
SADDLERS, ROPEMAKERS,
MUSICIANS, ROME,
MISSIONARY BISHOPS,
AND LAY PEOPLE.

Christians. To stop a riot, the Roman governor had Paul arrested. Paul insisted on his right as a Roman citizen to receive a trial in the capital of the empire, Rome itself. The ship taking him there was wrecked, and he spent two years in Malta. However, he was finally taken to Rome and spent some time under house arrest. There is evidence that he traveled again before he was beheaded during the persecution of Christians by the emperor Nero. By then, however, Paul had fulfilled his destiny. In his lifetime he had done more than anyone else to spread the Word among the Gentiles.

THOMAS
FIRST CENTURY

Thomas refused to believe that the other disciples had seen Jesus after the Crucifixion. Only when Jesus appeared again did Thomas believe.

"Because you have seen me, you have believed; blessed are those who have not seen and yet have believed."

THOMAS IS REMEMBERED as the disciple who was never afraid to speak his mind. When Lazarus, the brother of Mary and Martha, died, Jesus insisted on going to their house in the village of Bethany. This was dangerous because Bethany was near Jerusalem, from which Jesus had just been driven away. The other disciples were nervous, but not Thomas. If Jesus wanted to go, he was going, too, whatever the risk.

On another occasion, when the apostles were having supper with Jesus, he told them that he would be leaving them soon, but

This painting of Thomas shows him as a master craftsman. It was painted in the 16th century by Georges de la Tour. Thomas is regularly represented in art with a shovel, which refers to the stories of him traveling to India to build a palace for King Gundaphorus.

that they should not worry because they would know where he was (he meant heaven). Puzzled, Thomas asked Jesus to explain where he was going, and how they could follow him, and he answered: "I am the way, and the truth and the life; no one comes to the Father but by me." After the Resurrection, when Jesus first appeared to the apostles, Thomas was not with them. When the others told him about this, he did not believe them. For a week, "Doubting Thomas" refused to be persuaded, and then Jesus appeared again. He called upon Thomas to put his finger in the wounds on his hands and side. Thomas did, and then he believed.

A gospel said to have been written by Thomas was popular in medieval times. According to this, the apostles decided that each of them should spread the Gospel in a particular part of the world. Thomas was given the eastern world, including India. Thomas doubted that he could spread the gospel there, but the newly risen Jesus helped. The king of the Indians had sent an ambassador to Jerusalem to find a carpenter who could build him a magnificent house. Jesus pretended that Thomas was his slave and sold him to

the ambassador, who took him to India. Once there, Thomas had many adventures, and according to legend he died as a martyr. The Thomas Christians of southern India venerate Thomas as the founder of their church. Even though this is legendary, there is no doubt that the Thomas Christians have roots, dating back to the third century.

SAINT THOMAS IS THE PATRON SAINT OF THE EAST INDIES, PORTUGAL, ARCHITECTS, BUILDERS, SURVEYORS, MASONS, QUARRYMEN, AND CARPENTERS.

(Left) There are many different stories of Thomas' death. This painting shows his martyrdom at the hands of pagan priests.

JAMES AND JOHN
DIED C.44   DIED C.100

(*Right*) Saint John is shown here writing his gospel. The raven is one of his symbols.

SAINT JOHN IS THE PATRON SAINT OF WRITERS, BOOKBINDERS, AND FRIENDSHIP.
SAINT JAMES IS THE PATRON SAINT OF APOTHECARIES, BLACKSMITHS, CHILE, AND SPAIN.

JAMES AND JOHN were the sons of Zebedee and Salome, who was a sister of the Virgin Mary. They fished on Lake Genesareth, working with Andrew and Peter. Jesus nicknamed them the "sons of thunder," because they were a quick-spirited, hot-tempered pair. Jesus chose the sons of Zebedee, as well as Peter, to be with him at the Transfiguration. They were near him during his agony in the Garden of Gethsemane. All of the apostles were chosen, but John is said to have been the disciple whom Jesus loved most. John sat beside Jesus at the Last Supper, and when Jesus was dying on the cross, he asked John to look after his mother.

After the Resurrection, John, James, and Peter were leaders of the Jewish Christians in Jerusalem. Later, as a way of stopping him from preaching against Jewish law, the authorities exiled John to the island of Patmos. He spent his old age in Ephesus in Greece, which is where, according to tradition, he passed on his memories of Jesus and his teachings in the shape of the fourth gospel. The Gospel According to John begins with the resounding declaration: "In the beginning was the Word, and the Word was with God, and the Word was God." It concentrates on the teachings of Jesus and does not go into the details of his birth and childhood. By then, John was too frail to preach for long; and when people asked him for guidance on Christian commandments he simply told them to love one another.

James, John's brother, was the first apostle to be martyred. In the year 44, while he was in Jerusalem, he was beheaded on the orders of King Herod Agrippa I. According to an early story, one of his enemies was so sorry for having brought about his arrest that he became a Christian and was executed with James.

After the seventh century, James was particularly associated with Spain, where it was believed that he had preached. The shrine of James at Santiago de Compostela in northwestern Spain was, with Rome, Jerusalem, and Canterbury, one of the most important pilgrimage centers in medieval Europe. Pilgrims who had been to Santiago de Compostela went home with souvenir cockleshell badges, the emblem of James.

MATTHEW, MARK, AND LUKE

"Since I myself have carefully investigated everything from the beginning, it seemed good to me to write an orderly account for you, so that you may know the certainty of the things you have been taught."

Luke

THE PEOPLE WHO HAD KNOWN JESUS in his lifetime, heard his teachings, and witnessed his death and the Resurrection passed on what they knew by word of mouth. Their everyday language was Aramaic, but the languages of learning were Hebrew and Greek. From the middle of the first century, the gospels were recorded on papyrus scrolls. The writers, Matthew, Mark, Luke, and John, are called evangelists.

It is likely that Matthew wrote the first gospel. Matthew was working as a tax collector in Capernaum when Jesus called him to be an apostle. It seems that his gospel, which was intended for reading aloud, was first written in Hebrew, probably because after the Resurrection Matthew was living and preaching among the

(*Right*) A stained glass window from Chartres in France displaying Saint Matthew with a quill and an angel.

(*Below*) Saint Mark works on his gospel with a lion at his feet. The lion symbolizes this saint.

This painting of Saint Luke shows him as a learned and gentle scholar. The bull in the bottom right hand corner is Luke's emblem.

Jewish Christians of Judaea. Scholars believe that Mark and Luke knew of Matthew's work before they started their gospels.

Mark is said to have been in the Garden of Gethsemane when Jesus was arrested. He was so frightened that he ran away. He accompanied Paul on the first missionary journey, and then went on to Cyprus. After that, he found his way to Rome, where he met Paul again and acted as Peter's interpreter. While in Rome Mark wrote his gospel, which gives a full account of Peter's time with Jesus. Tradition says that Mark was martyred in Alexandria during the reign of Emperor Trajan, but he is the patron saint of Venice, because his relics were moved there in 829.

Unlike the other evangelists, Luke was a gentile. He was a doctor and a close friend of Paul's. He accompanied Paul on his second and third missionary journeys. Luke probably wrote his gospel after Paul's death, when he was living in Greece. Although Luke was too young to have known Jesus, his gospel contains some of the best-loved scenes of the New Testament, such as Mary's Magnificat, the parables of the Good Samaritan and the Prodigal Son.

SAINT MATTHEW IS
THE PATRON SAINT OF
TAX COLLECTORS AND
ACCOUNTANTS.
SAINT MARK IS
THE PATRON SAINT OF
STAINED GLASS MAKERS,
LAWYERS AND CAPTIVES.
SAINT LUKE IS
THE PATRON SAINT OF
DOCTORS, PAINTERS, LACE-
MAKERS, AND BUTCHERS.

Christopher is shown in this painting by Titian to be an enormously strong man. He uses a tree as a staff to help him cross the river. The traditional association between Saint Christopher and the protection of travelers is reflected in the continuing popularity of Saint Christopher medals and figurines, which are often seen in cars.

CHRISTOPHER AND VERONICA

THE ONLY HISTORICAL THING known about Christopher is that he was martyred in the third century. The tale of how he became the patron saint of travelers comes to us from *The Golden Legend*, a collection of saints' stories that was widely read and heard in medieval times.

Christopher was a giant who used his brute strength to bully people until he began to have visions of a cross. He did not understand what they meant until a hermit explained who Jesus Christ was and how he had died. Christopher was terribly sorry, but he despaired of ever making up for the violence of his past life. The hermit suggested that he could carry travelers over the rough water of a nearby river. So Christopher built himself a hut beside the river. For years, he carried travelers across the river. Then one terrible night, a mighty voice called him from his hut. He was amazed when he opened the door and saw a small boy. He lifted the boy up on to his shoulders, grasped his staff, and stepped into the stormy river. The boy was much heavier than he had expected, but even when the river was swirling around his face, he still pressed forward. At last, he reached the opposite bank. "Praise God," he gasped. "It seemed like I was carrying the weight of the whole world on my shoulders."

"So you did," said the boy, "for you have carried him who carries the sins of the whole world on your shoulders tonight. From now on, you will be called Christopher, the Christ-bearer." Then the boy told Christopher to stick his staff into the ground. The next morning, it had become a beautiful tree, bearing flowers and fruit.

Like Christopher, Veronica is a legendary saint. Her name means "true image," and she is said to have been a kind woman of Jerusalem who took pity on Jesus as he made his way along the Via Dolorosa, the path of pain, toward Calvary. As he fell under the weight of his cross, she wiped his face with her veil, which was stained with the imprint of his face.

The legendary Saint Veronica holds up the linen veil bearing the imprint of Christ's face, in a painting by the 16th-century artist El Greco.

SAINT VERONICA IS THE PATRON SAINT OF LAUNDRY WORKERS. SAINT CHRISTOPHER IS THE PATRON SAINT OF TRAVELERS AND PORTERS.

EARLY MARTYRS

This painting shows the stoning of Saint Stephen around the year 35. He died for asserting that Jesus was the Messiah for whom the Jews had been waiting. It is said that as he was stoned he saw a vision of Jesus sitting at God's right hand.

FOR CENTURIES Christians have been inspired by the courage of the martyrs, but the most moving of the stories that have come down to us are the ones told in their own words. Ignatius, who died in 107 during the reign of Trajan, was the bishop of Antioch when he was condemned to be killed by wild beasts. He wrote letters to Christians in other towns while he was being taken, under armed guard, to the Coliseum in Rome. Some of them wanted to rescue him. Instead Ignatius told them, "Be steadfast in the faith for their error; be gentle for their cruelty, and do not seek to retaliate." He regarded his approaching martyrdom as a privilege.

Perpetua and Felicity, two young women, were martyred with four male companions in 203 in the amphitheater at Carthage, in North Africa. Perpetua, who wrote an account of her imprisonment, was 22, married, and of noble birth. She was not afraid of dying for her faith, but she worried about her baby son and was sorry for the distress that her decision caused her pagan father. While she was in prison, Perpetua was encouraged by powerful visions. She saw a ladder leading to heaven and wrestled a demon to the ground. Felicity was a slave girl, who had a baby while she was in prison. Both of these women handed their babies to the care of friends and relations, and went into the huge amphitheater with joyful faces. "You judge us, God will judge you!" they shouted at the presiding official. The men with them faced a bear, a leopard, and a boar. A fierce wild cow was sent in against Felicity and Perpetua. After its first charge, they helped one another to their feet, and then, because they were not dead, gladiators were sent in to kill them with swords. When the first blow failed to kill her, Perpetua steadied the swordsman's aim with her own hand. "Perhaps," the writer of the martyrs' story said, "so great a woman, feared by the unclean spirit, could not have been slain unless she so willed it."

(*Above*) Saint Agnes was martyred by the sword around 305 because of her dedication to Jesus. Her emblem in paintings is a lamb.

(*Left*) A mosaic of Perpetua found in Ravenna, Italy. Her elaborate headdress and dress reveal her as a wealthy noblewoman.

"I am God's wheat. May I be ground by the teeth of the wild beasts until I become the fine wheat bread that is Christ's. My passions are crucified, there is no heat in my flesh. A stream flows murmuring inside me; deep down in me it says: Come to the Father."
Ignatius of Antioch

THE ROMAN EMPIRE

At its greatest extent, during the second century, the Roman Empire included all the land around the Mediterranean Sea and stretched as far as Britain in the northwest and Arabia in the southwest. Many different peoples speaking many different languages lived within this vast empire's boundaries, but there was a common law, and educated people knew Latin or Greek. The cities and towns of the empire were linked by long straight roads. These roads were built by the Roman army, but traders used them as much as soldiers, and in time Christian missionaries would travel along them.

Within the Roman Empire a variety of

J.M.W. Turner's painting of the temple of Jupiter, one of the Roman gods, with worshippers dancing in the fields below.

local religions were tolerated, as long as they did not interfere with the ceremonies of the official state religion. The official religion focused on the cults of gods, such as Jupiter and Mars, and goddesses, such as Juno and Vesta. Dead emperors were also regarded as gods. Animals were slaughtered and sacrificed to honor these deities, but no one loved them, or looked to them for answers about the purpose of life. By the time of Christ, foreign religions with more emotional and moral depth were spreading across the Roman Empire. The cult of the Persian bull-slaying

Christianity was finally accepted by the Roman Empire when Emperor Constantine converted and was baptized into the Church.

god, Mithras, appealed to soldiers because of its emphasis on brotherly love, while the cult of the Egyptian mother goddess Isis was popular among Roman women. The cult of a sun god, Sol Invictus, the Unconquered Sun, was sponsored by the Emperor Aurelian. The festival of Sol Invictus was celebrated on December 25, a date that was eventually borrowed by the Christians.

A strict Roman law forbade burial within the city walls, so the cemeteries were built between the hills and by the side of the roads outside. The word "catacomb" comes from the Latin for "near the hollow." Romans of all faiths were buried in the underground catacombs, but because burial places were protected, they were also used as refuges by early Christians. The rituals of the Christians aroused suspicion, which sometimes led

to persecution. To the Romans the communion meals, in which "flesh and blood" were eaten, sounded like cannibalism, and the "kiss of peace"

Underground cemeteries, or catacombs, outside the city of Rome, where the early Christians gathered.

that Christians exchanged seemed immoral. But for much of the time the early Christians did not have to live in fear. In the three hundred years before the reign of the emperor Constantine, which is when Christianity became an officially approved religion, there were ten periods of persecution. They tended to happen at times of crisis, during the reigns of weak emperors, such as Nero, Domitian, Caligula, and Septimus Severus.

In 313 the emperor Constantine's Edict of Milan granted freedom of worship to Christians. From then on, the Christian Church flourished. Constantine rebuilt the old Greek city of Byzantium (Istanbul) and renamed it Constantinople. From the time of its foundation, the new capital of the Eastern Roman Empire was a purely Christian city. In time, as the Western Roman Empire, with its capital of Rome, broke up under the impact of barbarian invasions, Constantinople became the center of the Greek-speaking Orthodox Christian Church, which spread into Russia.

ANTONY OF EGYPT

C.251–354

SAINT ANTONY IS THE PATRON SAINT OF GRAVE DIGGERS, DOMESTIC ANIMALS, BUTCHERS, BRUSH MAKERS, AND THE ORDER OF SAINT ANTONY.

ANTONY OF EGYPT is regarded as the first Christian hermit. By the fourth century, when Christians were no longer a struggling minority, men like him were searching for more challenging ways of coming close to God. At the age of 20, Antony sold everything he owned and went to live with a community of monks in the rocky desert of upper Egypt. These early Egyptian monks lived as simply as possible, devoting most of their time to prayer and meditation. After 15 years with them, Antony moved even farther away, to live as an anchorite, a solitary monk.

Alone in an abandoned fort in the mountains, Antony grappled with evil. The devil visited him in the form of hideous beasts, women, and soldiers, but he kept his faith and his mind unscathed. He never washed and his only friends were birds and animals. In spite of his longing for solitude, he could not remove himself entirely from the world. The other monks needed him as their spiritual leader. He had many visitors, people who were desperate for his advice, and he never turned anyone away. In 311 he even traveled to the city of Alexandria to lend moral support to the Christians who were confused by the doctrine of a priest called Arius, according to whom Jesus was not a divine being. The letters that are said to have been written by Antony show that, for all the severity of his own way of life, he was a sensible, moderate man.

Antony lived to be about 113. He insisted on being buried in a secret place, so that no one would make a fuss of his grave. But about 150 years later, his grave was found and his relics moved, first to Alexandria and later to Constantinople. By then Antony of Egypt was famous. His triumph over the forces of evil became a favorite subject of artists, and his "flight from the world" inspired many people, most notably Saint Augustine of Hippo, who said it influenced his conversion. Antony's monasticism inspired many imitators. European monks lived as hermits in isolated and inhospitable places where they could hope to find closeness to God.

(*Right*) This painting by the 17th-century painter David Teniers the Younger shows some of the trials Antony had to endure alone.

MARTIN OF TOURS

c.316–397

In this stained glass window created in the 16th century, Martin is ridding the countryside of beasts and serpents.

MARTIN WAS BORN in a small town near the Danube and spent his childhood in the places where his father, an officer in the Roman army, was stationed. When he was 15, he joined the army. One bitterly cold day, when he was riding through the town of Amiens in Gaul (France), he noticed a wretched beggar shivering by the side of the road. On an impulse, Martin pulled off his warm soldier's cloak and cut it in two with his sword. Then he dropped half over the beggar and went on his way. That night he had a dream in which he saw Jesus in heaven among the angels, and Jesus was wearing a soldier's cloak cut in half. This powerful dream was the turning point for Martin. He did not think he could serve God as a military man, but it was not easy to leave the army. When he refused to fight, his comrades called him a coward, even when he volunteered to stand unarmed in front of the Roman army's barbarian enemies. After a period in prison, Martin was free to start a new life as a Christian monk.

Martin spent his first years as a monk in Italy. He lived in a cave and relied on roots and herbs for his food. The shyest creatures, birds and squirrels, came right up to the mouth of his cave, and he is said to have rescued a hare from some hunters and nursed it back to health. In 360, Saint Hilary of Poitiers asked him to come to France, so that he could help him to spread Christianity among the Franks, the barbarian people who were settling around the Loire valley. At that time, Christianity had not spread much beyond the towns which the Romans had started.

Martin founded the first monastery in France, and even when he became the Bishop of Tours, he continued to live in a hermit's cell. His work as a missionary took him all over the region. He traveled by donkey and boat, and started many new monasteries in the communities which he had visited as a healer and preacher. Although Martin did not hesitate to destroy pagan shrines and

idols, he did not believe in forcing people to become Christians, and did his best to stop a local ruler from executing some heretics.

Martin was away from Tours when he died at the age of 80. Huge crowds flocked to his funeral, and it is said that as the barge carrying his body into Tours floated upstream, the trees on both banks burst into blossom, even though it was November. The feast of Saint Martin is celebrated all over northern Europe, partly because his life was written by his friend, Sulpicius Severus. Often he is shown with a goose, because geese migrate in November.

The famous scene of Martin sharing his cloak with a beggar painted by an unknown artist in the 15th century.

"Lord, if I am still necessary to your people, I do not refuse the work; may your will be done."

NICHOLAS

DIED C.345–352

A LL WE KNOW for certain about Nicholas, is that he was the bishop of Myra, a town in Asia Minor (now Turkey), in the fourth century. Five hundred years later, the story of his life was written down by Saint Methodius, and ever since he has been widely celebrated as the patron saint of sailors and children. Nicholas' most famous miracles involve threes: three girls, three boys, three sailors, and three prisoners. He saved the girls from the streets by giving each of them a bag of gold which they used as marriage dowries. He brought the boys back to life after they had been chopped into pieces by an innkeeper and dropped into a tub of salted water. He rescued

the sailors from a stormy sea, and he saved the lives of three men who had been unjustly condemned, by appearing

(Above) Nicholas flies through the skies to save a ship in this 14th-century painting by Lorenzo de Bicci.

to the emperor in a dream and persuading him to show mercy.

Late in the 11th century, Greek sailors brought Nicholas' relics from Myra to Bari in Italy, where they have remained. In many European countries, presents are given to children on Nicholas' feast day, December 6. In time, the Sinte Klaas of the Dutch people who settled in North America became Santa Claus, or Father Christmas.

SAINT NICHOLAS IS THE
PATRON SAINT OF RUSSIA, CHILDREN,
GREECE, BRIDES, FISHERMEN,
AND INNKEEPERS.

BASIL

c.330–379

BASIL came from a family of saints, including his father, his grandmother, Macrina the Elder, his sister, Macrina the Younger, and two of his brothers, Gregory of Nyssa and Peter of Sebaste. He grew up on the country estate of his grandmother in Cappadocia (now Turkey). She taught him the scriptures, but he also studied in the nearby city of Caesarea, in Athens, and in Constantinople, the capital of the Byzantine empire. On his return home he was heavily influenced by his sister Macrina and a great friend, Gregory of Nazianzus, and decided to become a monk.

Macrina had founded a monastery for women on the banks of a nearby river. After he had spent some time among the monks of Syria and Egypt, Basil founded a monastery for

"Finished and perfected, so far as we are able, is the mystery of thy incarnate work, O Christ our God.
For we have kept the memorial of thy death, we have seen the figure of thy resurrection, we have been filled with thine unending life, we have rejoiced in thine unfailing joy. Grant that we may be counted worthy of that same joy also in the age to come."

men on the opposite bank of the same river. He drew up the rules by which the monks and nuns lived. They took vows of poverty, chastity, and obedience, which meant that they had to live as simply as possible, remain unmarried, and obey their spiritual leader, or abbot. This rule was flexible enough to allow the monks to help the wider community by running hospitals and guest houses.

Before long Basil became the bishop of Caesarea, the town that developed around his monastery. As a bishop, Basil was an energetic participant in the controversies of the day. For example, some churchmen wanted pagan literature to be banned, but Basil regarded the ancient classics as a valuable part of a Christian education. He died when he was 49, worn out by fever, but he is seen as a positive influence on Greek monasticism.

Basil is represented in this 14th-century mural (wall painting), which can be found in Istanbul, Turkey.

SAINT BASIL IS THE PATRON SAINT OF HOSPITAL ADMINISTRATORS AND THE ORDER OF SAINT BASIL.

AUGUSTINE

354–430

The 19th-century artist Ary Scheffer portrays Augustine hand-in-hand with his beloved mother, Monica.

SAINT AUGUSTINE IS THE PATRON SAINT OF BREWERS, PRINTERS, CARTHAGE, AND THEOLOGIANS.
SAINT MONICA IS THE PATRON SAINT OF WIVES, WIDOWS, ALCOHOLISM, AND MOTHERS.

AUGUSTINE was born in Roman North Africa. Although his mother, Saint Monica, was a Christian, his father was a pagan. Augustine was an exceptionally clever pupil, who did so well at his first schools that his father sent him to the university city of Carthage. There he studied philosophy and law, but instead of getting a good job in the imperial service, he became one of the most brilliant teachers in Carthage. For 15 years he lived with a woman, and before he was 20 they had a son, whom he

named Adeodatus. Carthage was not big enough for a man of Augustine's talent and ambition. By the time he was 33, he was professor of rhetoric in Milan, the imperial city of northern Italy.

Saint Ambrose, the Bishop of Milan, was also a leading intellectual. Until he met Ambrose, Augustine regarded Christianity as a simple faith for good, but uneducated folk such as his own beloved mother, Monica. But Ambrose had a head as well as a heart, and he knew pagan philosophy as well as he knew the scriptures. Augustine was impressed by Ambrose, but he still didn't become a fully committed Christian. Monica had joined him in Milan, and she wanted him to settle down and marry the daughter of an important family. This was Augustine's situation when, as he was sitting in a garden, he heard a child singing, "Take up, read!" ("Tolle, lege!"). When he took up the nearest book, Saint Paul's *Epistles*, he was sure that God had called him to serve. Soon afterward, he was baptized by Ambrose and then returned to Africa with his mother, his friends, and his son. Sadly, Monica died on the way.

Back in Africa, Augustine divided his inheritance among the local poor and turned the family house into a center of prayer and study. In 395 he became the bishop of the sea port of Hippo (in present-day Algeria). He was loved by his flock, but proof of his saintliness derives from his writings. His most influential books are his *Confessions*, the story of his life up to his conversion, and *The City of God*, which grapples with the relationship between the sinful human world and divine creation.

Augustine supported the expulsion from the Church of heretics such as followers of the monk Pelagius, who preached that people can take the first steps to salvation without the grace of God. At the same time, he was sympathetic to women, especially mothers, and he never claimed to be anything but a sinner himself. "Love the sinner, hate the sin!" is one of his most famous sayings. When Augustine was on his deathbed, his last message was a reminder to his flock that they had been baptized in hope, and that whatever catastrophes befell them, they had been promised God's mercy.

An image of Augustine as the bishop of Hippo. He carries a crosier and the church building in his hands. The painting is by El Greco.

37

PATRICK

387–C.464

An illustration from this medieval text shows Patrick accidentally stabbing the king's son with his crosier.

"Christ be with me, Christ before me, Christ behind me...Christ in the heart of everyone who thinks of me, Christ in the mouth of everyone who speaks of me."

PATRICK was 16 when Irish pirates snatched him from his British homeland and sold him into slavery. For six years he watched over the sheep of his pagan master, consoling himself on the cold mountainside with prayers. Then he had a vision in which God told him to walk for 200 miles and find the ship that would take him back to civilization.

After his escape, Patrick was haunted by the voices of the pagan Irish, pleading with him to return with the Christian message. He became a priest, but partly because of his years in slavery, he was not educated enough to be made a bishop and sent back to Ireland by the pope as a missionary. However, he knew the native language, and he did not give up. So, around 430, he did return to Ireland as a bishop.

In order to move among the ordinary people Patrick first had to convert the royal families. To do that, he had to compete with the druids. According to legend, his miracles defeated their magic. One of his best known miracles was that he drove all the snakes away from Ireland. For all this wonder-working, Patrick was a down-to-earth bishop. At the baptism of a royal family, he accidentally jabbed his crosier into the foot of the king's son. Afterward, the man told him that he did not complain in case his wound was part of the rite. Such stories reveal that Patrick was trusted. By the time he died, the faith was well rooted in Ireland.

SAINT PATRICK IS THE PATRON
SAINT OF IRELAND
AND SNAKEBITES.

COLUMBA

521–597

COLUMBA, or Columcille, was born in Donegal in northwestern Ireland. His family was descended from a famous pagan king, Niall of the Nine Hostages, but he was dedicated to Christianity from a very early age. After spending some time as the foster son of a priest, he studied under the most famous abbots in Ireland, eventually founding new monasteries at Derry, Kells, and Durrow. In 563 he set sail with 12 monks and founded a new monastery on the island of Iona, off the western coast of Scotland. By all accounts, Columba was a brilliant scribe. According to one tradition, Columba was exiled as penance for having copied another monk's book of psalms (psalter) without permission, leading to a battle in which many lives were lost. Another early historian simply says, "he sailed away wishing to be an exile for Christ."

"Be thou a bright flame before me, be thou a guiding star above me, be thou a smooth path below me, be thou a kindly shepherd behind me, today, tonight, and forever."

From Iona, Columba acted as a spiritual adviser to the unruly Christian chieftains of western Scotland, and a missionary among the still pagan Pictish people. He died on the altar steps of his island abbey, having just copied the verse of Psalm 34: "They that seek the Lord shall want no good thing." That same year, Augustine of Canterbury started the Roman mission in southern England, but Iona continued to be the center of Christianity for Scotland and northeast England. In 635 King Oswald of Northumbria asked the monks at Iona for help in spreading Christianity among his people. So one of them, Aidan, left Iona and founded the island monastery of Lindisfarne.

This modern stained glass window depicting Columba is set in Iona Abbey. It was created by William Wilson.

SAINT COLUMBA IS THE PATRON SAINT OF POETS, SCOTLAND, AND IRELAND.

BENEDICT

c.480–547

"Listen carefully, my child, to your master's precepts, and incline the ear of your heart. Receive willingly and carry out effectively your loving father's advice, that by the labor of obedience you may return to Him from whom you had departed by the sloth of disobedience."

Benedict is shown praying with his monks in this 15th-century wall painting (fresco) from the Abbey of Monteoliveto Maggiore, Siena, Italy.

BENEDICT was a rich student living in Rome when, depressed by city life, he moved to the valley of Subiaco, about 40 miles away, to join the monks who had already retired there. Benedict's first cave was so remote that his food had to be lowered to him on a rope. According to legend he was fed by a raven, and when he was troubled by temptations, he would throw himself into a thorn bush. In spite of this harsh lifestyle, Benedict was a wise hermit. He founded several monasteries, including Monte Cassino, where the monks lived according to strict but sensible rules.

For Benedict, to work was to pray. His monks spent about four hours a day in church, four hours in private prayer and study, and six hours in the fields and workshops that kept the community in food and clothes. The emphasis was on order and calmness. Silence was encouraged. In summer, siestas were allowed, and the early morning service began slowly so that the "sleepyheads" would get there in time.

In his own lifetime, Benedict was regarded as a saintly man. He was buried in the same grave as his sister, Saint Scholastica. Most of our information about Benedict comes from his life story, which was written by Gregory the Great, another Benedictine.

SAINT BENEDICT IS THE PATRON SAINT OF BENEDICTINES, EUROPE, COPPERSMITHS, SCHOOLCHILDREN, AND THE DYING

GREGORY THE GREAT

c.540–604

GREGORY THE GREAT was born in Rome, where his father was a senator. He studied law and became the chief magistrate of the city. When his father died, he became a wealthy man, but he chose to give generously to the poor and to fund several Benedictine monasteries. He became the abbot of a Benedictine monastery in Rome and would have stayed there if the pope had not asked him to be his ambassador to the Byzantine imperial capital of Constantinople.

"Cleanse the thoughts of our hearts by the inspiration of thy Holy Spirit, that we may perfectly love thee, and worthily magnify thy holy name."

In 590, while plague was raging in Rome and the Lombards, a barbarian people, were invading Italy, Gregory himself reluctantly became pope. He is called "Great" because of the way in which he handled the crisis, and steered the Western Church's survival. Gregory organized the defense of Rome and negotiated a peace settlement with the Lombards. He bought corn for the poor, gave pensions to distressed aged senators, and reestablished contact with the churches of Gaul, Africa, and Spain, which had been cut off from Rome by the barbarian invasions. In 597, he sent a monk from his own Roman

Gregory is credited with freeing the city of Rome from the plague. Through his prayers, the Roman people survived.

monastery, Augustine of Canterbury, to convert the Anglo-Saxons. Gregory had a keen sense of justice. He did not allow the Jews to be ill-treated. Plainsong music is called "Gregorian Chant" because Gregory founded a school of sacred music.

SAINT GREGORY IS THE PATRON SAINT OF PUPILS, SCHOOLS, CHORISTERS, MUSICIANS, MASONS, AND SINGERS.

BEDE

c.673–735

THE "VENERABLE BEDE" was the most admired Englishman in medieval Europe, even though he never left Northumbria. He was only seven when he entered the monastery school at Durham, and from there he went to Jarrow, where, at 19, he was ordained as a priest. Although he belonged to a monastic community, reading and writing were, in his own words, his "special delight." During his years at Jarrow, he wrote many scientific, theological, and historical works.

"O God that art the only hope of the world,
The only refuge for unhappy men,
Abiding in the faithfulness of heaven,
Give me strong succor in this testing place."

Bede's *History of the English Church and Its People* is an exciting account of the development of the English Church. It brings to life many crucial occasions, such as the conversion of King Edwin of Northumbria in 625. Before he gave up the old gods, the king wanted to know what the Christian God could do for him. According to Bede, one of the courtiers persuaded the king to take a different attitude by comparing human existence to a sparrow in winter, flying through the door at one end of a warm banqueting hall and out through the door at the other end. "So," this nobleman said to Edwin, "this life of man appears for

Within a hundred years of Bede's death no monastic library worth its name was without copies of his works.

a short space, but of what went before, or what is to follow, we are completely ignorant. If, therefore, this new doctrine contains something more certain, it seems justly to deserve to be followed."

When he died, the Venerable Bede was mourned far beyond Northumbria. Saint Boniface said it was as though the candle of the Church had been extinguished.

BONIFACE

C.680–754

BONIFACE, the "Apostle of the Germans," was an Englishman. He was born in Devon in southwestern England, and his parents belonged to the Saxon nobility. He was a monk and a teacher before he was ordained at the age of 30, and soon afterward his abbot gave him permission to preach Christianity in Friesland.

This first mission lasted a couple of years, but Boniface had such an impact that the pope agreed to his request to take Christianity to the other German-speaking tribes and to organize their Church.

Boniface was an unstoppable, fearless missionary. On one famous occasion, he took an ax to the Geismar Oak, a tree that was sacred to Thor, the pagan god of thunder. At the first stroke of his ax, God sent down a mighty wind that felled the oak, which broke into the shape of a cross. Wherever he went, Boniface founded monasteries, many of which were staffed by monks and nuns from England. In later life, Boniface returned to Friesland, only to be killed by pagans at a gathering of his new converts.

Boniface means "Speaker of Good News," but he was christened Wynfrith which means "joy and peace."

SAINT BONIFACE IS THE PATRON SAINT OF BREWERS AND TAILORS.

CYRIL AND METHODIUS

C.827–869   *C.826–885*

A window at Saint Vitus' cathedral in Prague shows the brothers Cyril and Methodius praying.

Methodius became an abbot, and Cyril went back to teaching.

In 862 the ruler of what is now Slovakia asked the Patriarch of Constantinople (the Eastern Church's equivalent of the pope) for a bishop who could teach his people in their own language. Cyril and Methodius were well suited to this job. They invented an alphabet,

"The Slavs were happy because they listened to the great deeds of God in their own tongue."

from which we get the "Cyrillic" script, and they translated the gospels into it. When they also translated the liturgy, the words used in divine service, they ran into problems because some other bishops insisted that Hebrew, Greek, and Latin were the only sacred languages. The brothers went to Rome to get the pope's approval for their Slavonic liturgy.

Cyril died while he was in Rome, but Methodius returned to Slovakia. In time he had translated the whole Bible into Slavonic, and drawn up laws for his converts. He died in his cathedral, and his feast-day is the same as Cyril's, February 14. Unusually, the brothers worked with the approval of both the Roman and Greek churches.

SAINTS CYRIL AND METHODIUS ARE THE PATRON SAINTS OF EUROPE.

CYRIL AND METHODIUS were brothers, who became missionaries to the Slav people living along the Danube. Before he became a priest, Methodius had been the governor of a Slav-speaking province of the Byzantine Empire. Cyril, who was also a priest, had worked as a scholar in Constantinople. In 860 they took Christianity to the Khazars, the people living between the Don and Volga rivers. On their return,

WENCESLAS

907–929

WENCESLAS AND LUDMILLA were martyred during the turbulent early days of the Czech Church. Wenceslas, or Vaclav, was a prince, the son of the Duke of Bohemia, in the present-day Czech Republic. He was brought up by Saint Ludmilla, his devoutly Christian grandmother. Her influence over the young heir to the duchy was so resented by other members of the royal family that they murdered her. But when Wenceslas became Duke of Bohemia, he carried on in the spirit of his Christian grandmother, encouraging the religious and educational improvement of his people.

"Therefore Christian men be sure,
Wealth or rank possessing,
Ye who now will bless the poor,
Shall yourselves find blessing."

A few years after he became duke, Wenceslas himself was murdered. His brother Boleslav invited him to his house and started an argument with him. In the resulting fight Boleslav slew Wenceslas. It is hard to separate Wenceslas' fate from the politics of the time. His Christianity was one element in a power struggle between Bohemia's ruling families. Although some of these nobles were hostile to Christianity, most were angry because Wenceslas had allowed the German emperor to become the overlord of Bohemia.

The duke Wenceslas appears as a soldier in this 16th-century oil painting from the Czech Republic.

Within 50 years of his assassination, Wenceslas was regarded as Bohemia's patron saint. Later Czech kings were named after him, coins bore his portrait, and his tomb in Saint Vitus' Cathedral in Prague became an important shrine. The "Good King Wenceslas" of the famous carol, which was written by J.M. Neale in the 19th century, is only an imaginary relation of the saintly young duke.

STANISLAUS

1030–1079

STANISLAUS SZCZEPANOWSKI was the first Pole to be canonized. In 1072 he became bishop of Cracow and gained a reputation for his charity and his work as a reformer and preacher. Stanislaus was not afraid to criticize the unruly king, Boleslav II. After Stanislaus had excommunicated him for kidnapping the wife of one of his nobleman, Boleslav accused the troublesome bishop of treason.

The royal court found Stanislaus guilty of plotting with Poland's German neighbors to overthrow Boleslav and sentenced him to the loss of his limbs. According to tradition, the king's knights could not bring themselves to carry out this gruesome sentence, so Boleslav took the unjust law into his own hands. He stormed into Cracow's Church of Saint Michael, where Stanislaus was saying mass, and butchered him with his own sword.

After this outrage, Pope Gregory VII put the whole of Boleslav's realm under an interdict, which meant that the churches were closed to everyone. The interdict was lifted when Boleslav fell from power, by which time the murdered bishop was revered as a martyr. Stanislaus has a special place in Poland's history, and many of its later kings were named after him.

"O God, our Father in heaven, to honor You, Saint Stanislaus faced martyrdom with courage. Keep us strong and loyal in our faith until death."

Stanislaus staggers back, having been stabbed in the cathedral by the king, who rushes out.

ELIZABETH OF HUNGARY

1207–1231

ELIZABETH was a Hungarian princess, but she spent most of her life in Thuringia, a region of Germany. When she was only nine, she was betrothed to Prince Ludwig, the son of the ruler of Thuringia, and brought up at his court. Ludwig and Elizabeth were married when he succeeded his father. Although this marriage had been arranged, it was also a love match. The royal couple lived happily in the great castle at Wartburg, and they had three children. One famous story tells of a day when Elizabeth was hurrying out of the castle to give bread to the poor. When she bumped into her husband, the loaves in her arms turned into roses. This miracle suggests that Ludwig would not have been sympathetic, but in fact he supported her work with orphans and sick people.

Elizabeth not only gave food and clothing to the poor, she also cared for them when they were injured and sick.

SAINT ELIZABETH IS THE PATRON SAINT OF BAKERS, BEGGARS, WIDOWS, AND LACEMAKERS.

In 1227 Ludwig died on his way to a crusade. When Elizabeth heard the news, she was filled with grief. Her brother-in-law became Regent of Thuringia and made her leave the castle. She started living as a Franciscan nun in a small house near the hospital where she worked. Unfortunately, she was bullied by her spiritual director, Konrad of Marburg. No matter how cruel he was, Elizabeth recovered. She did anything for the people who depended on her, mending clothes, spinning, and cleaning. When she died, she was only 24. Four years later, the long-suffering princess was canonized.

THE MIDDLE AGES TO THE REFORMATION

THROUGHOUT THE MIDDLE AGES, the saints had a secure place in the devotions of Western Christians. The saints were close to God in heaven, and because they were already saved, their merits amounted to a "treasury of graces," a spiritual fund from which ordinary sinners could hope to benefit through prayer and good works.

From the 12th century on, European scholars were able to study the scriptures in Hebrew and Greek, as well as the science and philosophy of the pre-Christian classical world, which had been preserved by Byzantine, Jewish, and Muslim scholars. The centers of learning shifted from monasteries to universities, such as the one in Paris where

Monks bless the departure of crusaders. The medieval Church encouraged knights and princes to fight against Muslims.

Thomas Aquinas taught. This shift gave rise to a new, scientific spirit of inquiry and a new attitude to human earthly existence, which is called Humanism. Long known in China, printing was developed in Europe in the 1450s, making books more easily available. In the 15th century, these changes produced a great flowering in the arts and sciences, which is called the Renaissance (French for "rebirth").

Humanist scholars such as Thomas More and Erasmus of Rotterdam were eager to recapture the simplicity of the early Christians, and they were critical of the extravagant life style of the Church's leaders.

Pope Julius II lived as richly as a prince. In 1503 in order to finance the plan to demolish the old St. Peter's Church in Rome and replace it with a splendid new building, he and his successors launched a massive sale of indulgences, partial pardons for sins. This was one of the practices that concerned a German monk called Martin Luther. In 1517, he pinned a list of complaints against the Church on the door of the castle church in Wittenberg. He wanted to start a debate about reforming what he saw as a corrupt Church.

The Protestant Reformation which followed divided Christians in the Western Church, and led to centuries of violence and intolerance. For Protestants, salvation came only through faith in and knowledge of God.

(*Right*) Martin Luther, painted by Cranach, was concerned about the corruption of the Church, especially the sale of indulgences.

(*Below*) Saint Thomas More, here painted by Holbein, was a Renaissance scholar who was critical of Church leaders.

The words of holy scripture replaced the images and stories of the saints, and the authority of the pope was rejected.

After the upheavals of the Reformation, in the mid-16th century leading Catholic churchmen met at Trent in northern Italy to discuss changes in church policy. The reforms arising from this Council of Trent included an overhaul of the procedure for canonization. While saints continued to be made in the Catholic and Orthodox churches, in Protestant religions where their veneration was no longer encouraged, the saints lived on in people's hearts as folk heroes. Saint Nicholas, for example, evolved into Santa Claus.

HILDEGARD

1098–1179

The young Hildegard, kneeling on the left, is shown experiencing one of her many visions in this 15th-century painting.

SAINT HILDEGARD IS THE PATRON SAINT OF PHILOLOGISTS AND ESPERANTISTS.

HILDEGARD was the tenth child of the Count of Spanheim. She was eight when she went to live with her aunt Jutta, the abbess of the Benedictine convent of Diessenberg in Germany. When Jutta died, Hildegard became abbess. Ever since she was a toddler, Hildegard had been having revelations, visions in which God spoke to her. She had told no one but her aunt about them, but in 1141, when she was 43 years old, she received a divine command to record her visions. This command made her very ill, but the priest in charge of the convent encouraged her to go ahead.

Hildegard's first book, *Scivias*, "Know the Ways of the Lord," contained 26 astonishing visions, which were illustrated by Hildegard's own paintings. These visions dealt with every aspect of human existence, including the organization of the Church, God's relationship with all

the animals and plants, and ways in which people could be saved. A committee of theologians examined Hildegard's extraordinary book. They believed that since she had spent most of her life in a cloister, the brilliance of her writings could only be explained by her special relationship with God.

The Church's approval gave Hildegard confidence, and she became a celebrity. Despite her success, Hildegard was unhappy about the fact that men were in charge of convents. In 1147, acting on a vision that told her to found an independent house, she left Diessenberg with 18 of her nuns, and founded a convent at Rupertsberg, near Bingen.

Hildegard's visions were so powerful that they sometimes disabled her, but whenever she was well she was unstoppable. In addition to two more books of visions, several saints' lives, and a symphony of 77 hymns, she also wrote two scientific works, on medicine and natural history. These works contain ideas that were far ahead of Hildegard's times. For example, she suggested that the blood circulates around the body and that the brain sends its commands to the body via the nerves.

Until she was well into her 70s, Hildegard was active as an abbess and a preacher. After her death she was venerated in Germany, but it is only in recent times that Hildegard is esteemed as a saint with a heightened awareness of divine creation, a mystic to whom God's love was revealed as a nurturing and sustaining care.

Here, watched by her sister nuns, Hildegard records one of her powerful visions.

(*Left*) A monument showing the death of Christ located at the convent Hildegard established in Bingen, Germany.

"From my infancy up to the present time, when I am more than seventy years of age, I have always seen this light in my spirit....The light which I see...is more brilliant than the sun...and I name it the cloud of living light. And as the sun, moon, and stars are reflected in the water, so the scriptures and sermons, and virtues and works of men, shine in it before me."

THOMAS À BECKET

1118–1170

Thomas appears on the right in this 15th-century painting with Saint Martin of Tours.

(*Right*) Henry II, the young king whose angry words led to the murder of Thomas à Becket.

"I commend myself to God, Saint Mary, and all the saints of the church....For the name of Jesus and the protection of the church I am ready to embrace death."

THOMAS À BECKET was born in London. When he left school, after time as a clerk and a secretary, Thomas worked for the Archbishop of Canterbury, who arranged for him to study law in France and Italy. In 1155 the new king of England, Henry II, made Thomas his chief minister. Although Thomas was 15 years older than Henry, the two men were great friends. They always sat together, even in church, and they shared a passion for riding and hunting.

In 1162 Henry got Thomas appointed the Archbishop of Canterbury. He did not think that Thomas' new job would make any difference to their friendship, but Thomas had different ideas. Once he was Archbishop, Thomas changed from being "a patron of play-actors and a follower of hounds, to being a shepherd of souls." This change happened at a time when there was conflict between the Church and the State in several European countries. Kings wanted to control bishops, and bishops wanted to control kings. Nearly 100 years before Thomas' appointment, the pope had tried to stop kings from appointing bishops, but Thomas would not have been appointed without Henry's approval.

Henry was angry when Thomas insisted that bishops and the clergy were only answerable to the pope and God. He was angrier still when Thomas got in the way of his attempt to set up laws that would cover members of the clergy as well as his lay subjects. The argument between the former friends became so

serious that for his own safety Thomas left England. The pope intervened, and the two men patched up their differences, so Thomas returned to Canterbury. However, the dispute blew up again. On Christmas Eve in 1170, Thomas excommunicated those who disagreed with him and the Church. Henry was in Normandy at the time, and he exploded, saying, "Who will rid me of this turbulent priest?"

Henry had said things like that before, but this time four of his knights took him seriously. They crossed the Channel, rode to Canterbury, and murdered Thomas in a side chapel of the cathedral. Europe was shocked to learn of this atrocity. Henry, too, was horrified and came to Canterbury in a rough hair shirt to do penance for Thomas' death. Although Thomas had not lived as a saint, he died bravely in defense of the rights of the Church. Three years after his murder, he was canonized, and within another seven years no fewer than 703 miracles were credited to him. His shrine became one of the most important pilgrimage centers in Europe.

(*Top left*) Canterbury Cathedral as it looks today.

(*Above*) This image from a 13th-century illuminated manuscript shows the knights brutally killing Thomas in the side chapel.

SAINT THOMAS IS THE PATRON SAINT OF PORTSMOUTH AND OFFICIALS.

FRANCIS OF ASSISI

1181–1226

FRANCIS CAME FROM the town of Assisi in northern Italy, where his family was in the wool trade. He was christened Giovanni, but was called Francis because he was born when his father was away on business in France. He was a high-spirited, fashion-conscious teenager, with a talent for composing and singing romantic troubadour songs. None of his early friends would have expected him to become a monk.

When war broke out between Assisi and a neighboring town, Francis joined the army and was taken prisoner. Captivity and several illnesses caused him to rethink his life. Still looking for military glory, he joined a crusade, but a vision from God made him return home. One day, when he was visiting the half-ruined chapel of San Damiano, he heard a voice telling him, "Go and repair my house!" Francis immediately set about restoring San Damiano with his own hands. To the horror of his parents, who thought he had gone mad, he sold some of their most expensive cloth to pay for materials. Hoping to shame his son into sense, his father took him before the courts. In the main square of Assisi, Francis handed everything that he owned, even the clothes he was wearing, to his father, thereby giving up his inheritance.

From that day forward, Francis was in the service of God. He lived among the poorest of the poor, sleeping in haylofts, leper hospitals, and church porches, and relying on casual work and charity for his food. He preached in the language of ordinary people, praising all the creatures and phenomena of Creation. Once, when the townspeople of Gubbio were living in fear of a wolf, Francis went right up to the beast and asked it in the name of God to stop hurting people. To the amazement of onlookers, the wolf trotted forward and lay down at

The Italian town of Assisi where Francis was born and grew up. He and his followers used Assisi as a base from where they would travel to preach.

54

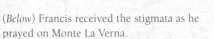

(*Above*) Many miracles are attributed to Francis. This painting shows him bringing a boy back from the dead. The woman at the head of the bed is Saint Clare, who founded the Poor Clares, Franciscan nuns.

(*Below*) Francis received the stigmata as he prayed on Monte La Verna.

the saint's feet. From then on, the wolf of Gubbio was as tame as a pet.

Other men joined Francis, and before long the wandering friars in the ragged brown habits were recognized as a "mendicant" (beggarlike) religious order. Francis traveled to Spain and made several attempts to convert the Muslims of North Africa. Francis aimed to live as simply as Jesus had, and in 1224, after an intense vision, he was marked with replicas of Christ's wounds, the stigmata. A year later, he composed his famous song, "The Canticle of Brother Sun," but by then he was in poor health. He was taken back to Assisi, where he refused to lie on a bed. Instead, he chose to die on the bare earth.

SAINT FRANCIS IS THE PATRON SAINT OF FRANCISCANS, ITALY, MERCHANTS, ANIMALS, AND ECOLOGISTS.

DOMINIC

*c.*1170–1222

Dominic is receiving the rosary and a lily from Our Lady in this 17th-century painting by Battista Pittoni. He wears the black and white habit of the Domincan order, as opposed to the brown habit of the Franciscans.

DOMINIC grew up in Spain. He studied at the University of Palencia and became a priest. In 1203, when he was traveling through France, he came into contact with Albigensian heretics. Since there was so much evil in the world, the Albigensians did not believe that there could be just one good Supreme Being. Instead, they believed in two rival beings or forces, evil and good. Good dominated the soul, and evil dominated the body, which meant that everything to do with the body was evil. As heretics, the Albigensians were terrorized for their beliefs, but Dominic was convinced that persuasion, not persecution, was the only way to win them back to Christianity.

With six companions, Dominic began to preach among the Albigensians. Like the Franciscans, the wandering Dominican friars took vows of poverty and lived on what they could beg. In 1215 Dominic met Francis, and they became friends. But Dominic was more of an organizer than Francis, and from the beginning his friars, who were more highly trained than the Franciscans, specialized in education. Dominic is said to had a vision in which Mary encouraged him and told him to pray the rosary. This tradition probably arose from his talent as a teacher. He liked to sing the psalms and liturgy and explained the mysteries of Christianity in ways that ordinary people could understand.

Dominic spent the last five years of his life organizing the new order, but died on his way to the pagans of Hungary. By then the Dominicans, nicknamed *Domini canes* ("hounds of the Lord"), were established in many of Europe's towns.

SAINT DOMINIC IS THE PATRON SAINT OF BOLOGNA IN ITALY, ASTRONOMERS, SCIENTISTS, AND THE DOMINICAN REPUBLIC.

CATHERINE OF SIENA

1347–1380

CATHERINE OF SIENA, a wealthy wool-dyer's daughter, was the last of 25 children. She refused to marry and became a Dominican sister. At first she spent most of her time on her own, sending herself into such intense trances that she heard the voice of God. Then, when she was 23, God told her to go out into the world, and within months she was the talk of Siena.

Catherine called for the renewal of the Church, and she was a sensational preacher. She never learned to write, but her followers wrote down her teachings. At that time the city-states of Tuscany, Catherine's part of Italy, were at war with the Papal states. The pope had moved to the French city of Avignon, where he was dominated by the French king. Catherine started a campaign for peace and the return of the pope.

In 1377 Pope Gregory XI came back to Rome, but soon afterward he died and his successor, Pope Urban VI, was challenged by another Avignon-based pope. Catherine

During her intense trances Catherine suffered the pain of the stigmata, the wounds of Christ, which are shown here.

"Catherine cried, 'O good and sweet Jesus, where wert thou while my soul was being so sorely tempted?' The answer came, 'I was in thy heart, Catherine, for I will not leave anyone who does not first leave me.'"

SAINT CATHERINE IS THE PATRON SAINT OF ITALY, SICKNESS, NURSES, AND FIREFIGHTERS.

dictated many letters to cardinals, urging them to support Urban. She was in Rome when she died suddenly. Although her role as a peacemaker has been exaggerated, her book of visions, the *Dialogue*, is regarded as a classic of mysticism.

THOMAS AQUINAS

C.1225–1274

THOMAS AQUINAS was the son of the count of Aquino. He was born in the family castle in southern Italy, near his first school, the famous monastery of Monte Cassino. At the University of Naples, Thomas was a brilliant student, and his parents expected him to become a great churchman. His mother was so angry when he decided to join the Dominicans, a begging order, that she had him locked up in the family castle. Eventually Thomas persuaded her to let him go to Paris and study under the Dominican scholar Albertus Magnus.

This was the period when European scholars were excited by the work of ancient Greek philosophers and Muslim scientists. Albertus Magnus was an expert on the philosophy of Aristotle. Thomas listened so much and said so little in class that his fellow students nicknamed him the "dumb ox," but Albertus Magnus said that the lowing of this particular ox would one day fill the world.

Philosophy then included areas of knowledge that have since divided into separate studies such as mathematics and physics. Aristotle had used logic, or reason, to describe the workings of the visible world. But this took no account of the invisible presence of God, which troubled many Christian scholars. Thomas took on the task of reconciling scientific logic with faith. He used Aristotle's methods to show that there were logical reasons for believing in the existence of God. One of his works, the *Summa Theologica*, became the basis of Catholic doctrine.

Since he spent most of his life studying and preaching and writing, Thomas' outward life was uneventful. The "angelic doctor" was

The famous Renaissance Italian painter Sandro Botticelli painted this portrait of Thomas Aquinas holding a book and quill.

"O victim slain for us and our salvation,
Opening the door of light,
The warring hosts are set on our damnation:
Give us the strength to fight."

SAINT THOMAS AQUINAS IS
THE PATRON SAINT OF
CATHOLIC SCHOOLS,
THEOLOGIANS, PUBLISHERS,
PENCIL MAKERS, AND BOOK
DEALERS.

tall and fat, and inclined to be rather absent-minded, though he was unfailingly courteous to his students. However, he was never satisfied with his academic work. In December 1273, while he was saying Mass, he had a mystical experience of such joy that he could not bring himself to finish the third part of the *Summa Theologica*. He told his secretary, "All I have written seems to me like so much straw compared with what I have seen and what has been revealed to me." A year later, he died on his way to a theological conference.

BIRGITTA OF SWEDEN

c.1303–1373

(*Right*) This painted wooden relief of
Birgitta sitting at her desk can be
found in the State History Museum in
Stockholm.

SAINT BIRGITTA IS THE
PATRON SAINT OF SWEDEN,
SCHOLARS, AND WIDOWS.

BIRGITTA (or Bridget) was 14 when she married Ulf
Godmarsson, a nobleman like her father. Ulf became the
governor of the Swedish province of Nericia, and he and
Birgitta had eight children. When she was about 32, Birgitta was
appointed as chief lady-in-waiting to Sweden's queen. While she
was at court she began to experience divine visions, overwhelming
images of the Virgin Mary and the Crucified Christ.

Birgitta went on pilgrimage to Spain with her husband, but in
1344, soon after their return, Ulf died. "When I buried my
husband," she said later, "I buried all my earthly
love with him, for though I loved him as my own
soul, I would not for a penny buy back his life
against the will of God." As a widow with grown
children, Birgitta felt free to devote her time to
prayer and penance at the Cistercian monastery
where her husband had spent his last days. She
confided her visions to the abbot, and he
translated them into Latin. While she was there,
she had a vision instructing her to start a new
religious order. She was such a
forceful and well-respected
character that King Magnus II
helped her to acquire the land and
the money she needed to set up her
first community at Vadstena. Sixty
nuns and 25 monks belonged to
Birgitta's Order of the Holy Savior,
known later as the Brigettines.

In 1350 Birgitta set out on the
long journey to Rome to obtain the
pope's approval for her order. Apart
from several pilgrimages including
one to the Holy Land, Birgitta spent
the rest of her life in Rome. She
started another Brigettine

community there. Besides their work among the poor and sick, the Brigettines took a special interest in the welfare of pilgrims, people who, like Birgitta herself, were far from home. Birgitta was a woman of energy and confidence. She had something to say and do about all the world's problems, whether they were moral, practical, or political. She was no theologian, but her preaching was enlivened by the power of her visions and her own experience as a mother. Like Catherine of Siena, Birgitta campaigned for the return of the pope from Avignon, but she died before she had his approval for the Brigettines. Some years after her death, her daughter Catherine gained this approval and returned to Sweden. Catherine became the abbess of Vadstena and was also venerated as a saint.

(*Left*) Birgitta traveled a great deal during her life—this image shows her on horseback.

(*Top*) Birgitta's shrine is in the Abbey church, Vadstena, which was built under her directions.

(*Above*) The convent Birgitta established was housed in a mansion built during the 13th century.

JOAN OF ARC
1412–1431

OR MORE than 500 years Joan of Arc, the peasant girl who had a huge impact on the history of France, has been revered as a heroine and a saint. While Joan was growing up, the French and English were battling for control of France. She was keenly aware of this conflict, the Hundred Years War, because Champagne, her native region, was controlled by the Burgundians, who were allies of the English.

Joan was 13 when she first became aware of "voices." They were the voices of the angel Michael and her favorite saints, Catherine of Alexandria and Margaret of Antioch, and sometimes she could see as well as hear them. They told her that she would play a decisive part in uniting her country under one French king. Although Joan could not read or write or ride a horse, she was so sure of that message that when she was 17 she went to see the local commander of the French forces. He did not take her seriously until, just as she had prophesied, the French army suffered another defeat. Next, Joan went to meet the dauphin Charles, the heir to the throne of France.

The dauphin allowed her to lead a troop of soldiers to the besieged city of Orleans. Her battle standard was emblazoned with the words "Jesus; Maria." Within a few months, the English army was in retreat, and in 1429 Joan stood by the dauphin's side as he was crowned Charles VII in the cathedral at Reims.

But the war continued, and when Joan fell into the hands of the Burgundians, they sold her to the English. While she was awaiting trial as a heretic and a witch, she was treated harshly. Throughout the trial, Joan insisted on her innocence, but her accusers knew that they could not afford to let her live. She was burned at the stake in Rouen. In her final agony, she called out to the saints who had inspired her, and her last word was a murmured "Jesus." Twenty five years later, Pope Callistus III declared her innocent of heresy and witchcraft, but it was not until 1920 that this brave and steadfast young woman was officially canonized.

(*Above*) Joan in prison being questioned by Cardinal Henry Beaufort.

(*Left*) Ingres' painting of Joan dressed as a warrior maiden at Charles VII's coronation.

SAINT JOAN IS THE PATRON SAINT OF FRANCE, MARTYRS, PRISONERS, AND SOLDIERS.

IGNATIUS LOYOLA

c.1491–1556

(*Above*) Rubens' painting of Ignatius as founder of the Jesuits.

(*Right*) Ignatius as a soldier.

SAINT IGNATIUS IS THE PATRON SAINT OF THE JESUITS, SOLDIERS, RETREATS, AND SPIRITUAL EXERCISES.

IGNATIUS LOYOLA was the youngest of twelve children. His family belonged to the Spanish nobility, and he became an army commander. In 1521, while recovering from a leg wound, he was given a life of Christ and the lives of the saints to read. These books had such an effect on him that he decided to devote the rest of his life to Christ.

He made a pilgrimage to the mountain monastery of Montserrat and laid his weapons down at the altar. After spending a night at the feet of Montserrat's statue of the Madonna, he walked to Manresa, where he spent nearly two years as a hermit. At Manresa, Loyola strengthened himself with spiritual exercises, periods of intense concentration on the central beliefs of the Catholic faith.

In 1523 Loyola begged his way to Jerusalem, where he realized that he would not be able to work as a missionary or a teacher if he did not know Latin. He returned to Spain and went back to school. By 1528 Loyola was in Paris, where he taught his spiritual exercises to his close friends. He was 43 when he received his master's degree from the University of Paris. In that same year, he banded together with six of his friends to form a "Society of Jesus." The following year all of them were ordained as priests.

Now, "for the greater glory of God," Ignatius Loyola's group volunteered for any task the pope might assign them. In 1540 the pope approved of them as a new religious order, the Society of Jesus, or Jesuits, and Ignatius Loyola was its first superior. They promised complete obedience to the pope and his successors, and they were dedicated to education and missionary work, "whether to the Turks or to the New World or to the Lutherans or to others, be they infidel or faithful." More than 7,000 of Loyola's letters and instructions have survived. His society grew into a thousand-strong organization, setting up schools, colleges, and seminaries in the cities of Western Europe, and sending missionaries across the oceans to the New World.

DICNACIO DE LOYOIA

65

FRANCIS XAVIER

1506–1552

SAINT FRANCIS XAVIER IS THE PATRON SAINT OF GOA IN INDIA, AND MISSIONS.

Francis sometimes walked through the streets of Goa with a handbell, which attracted children. They would gather to listen to stories about the saints and learn the Lord's Prayer and the Creed.

FRANCIS XAVIER was born in Navarre, in southwestern France. Instead of pursuing an academic career in Paris, he chose to follow his eccentric older friend, Ignatius Loyola, and join the revolutionary Jesuits. The Jesuits were especially committed to missionary work, and in 1541, Francis went to work in the Portuguese colony of Goa in India. The Europeans living in Goa were a poor advertisement for Christian virtues. Francis did his best to teach, and represent, a more just and charitable Christianity. The majority of his converts were poor people belonging to the lowest Hindu caste.

For the next seven years, Francis worked as a missionary in southern India, Sri Lanka, and the Malay peninsula. He was often seasick, and in one of his letters to Rome he complained about his right arm, because it ached from administering so many baptisms. Baptism was an urgent matter in those days because many Christians believed that unbaptized people would go to hell.

In August 1549 he reached Japan. Without a valuable gift, he was not allowed to see the Mikado (ruler) at Miyako. At Yamaguchi, he changed into splendid clothes and presented himself to the rulers bringing expensive gifts. He was then allowed to use an abandoned Buddhist monastery

Francis Xavier baptizes newly converted Christians as Saint Francis Borgia, another Jesuit missionary and preacher, prays for them.

The Chapel of Saint Francis Xavier in Goa, India, contains his remains in this casket. The chapel continues to be a place of pilgrimage.

as a base for his mission. Within two years there were about 2,000 Christians in Japan. While he was in Japan, he kept hearing about the Chinese empire. In 1552 he sailed from Goa on a secret mission to China, which was closed to outsiders. His ship was off the Chinese coast when he became seriously ill. He was carried to an island and died in the care of a young Chinese convert. His body was taken back to Goa, where miracles were claimed at his shrine.

TERESA OF AVILA

1515–1582

A 20th-century stained glass window in Saint Audries' Church, England, shows Teresa in the habit of a discalced Carmelite.

TERESA DE CEPEDA Y AHUMADA was born in Spain, the world superpower of the 16th century. Her family was wealthy and cultured, and every one of her seven brothers worked in the Spanish "New World" of South America. When Teresa was about 21, she entered a Carmelite convent, and it did not seem likely that she would play a major part in the great changes of her day.

Life at Teresa's convent was not too "monastic." The nuns, high-born ladies like Teresa, were free to wear their own clothes and entertain regular visitors, and they did not have to do any work. Within a year, Teresa became ill, and it got so bad that, in 1539, a grave was dug for her. Instead of dying, however, Teresa got better. She was strengthened by visions, journeys of the soul that gave her a sense of being directly in touch with God.

While she was recovering, she became increasingly dissatisfied with the easygoing routines of convent life. It seemed to her that the Carmelites had drifted from the challenging simplicity of their early rule. In 1562, inspired by a powerful vision, she began to reform the Carmelite Order. In that same year she set up her first convent, Saint Joseph's, in Avila. Her nuns were called "discalced" (shoeless) Carmelites because they wore sandals and rough brown habits.

In the next 20 years, Teresa of Avila traveled all over Spain and set up more than 20 reformed Carmelite convents. She had to deal with opposition from the unreformed Carmelites, who did not want to change their routines. To help her nuns, Teresa wrote her *Life* and several books, including *The Way of Perfection* and *The Interior Castle*. These books reveal her as a brilliant writer and a lively, likeable woman.

Teresa made a huge impact on everyone who met her, but she never thought of herself as a saint. "One of the things that makes me happy here," she wrote from her convent at Seville, "is that there is no

In this 17th-century painting by Claudio Coello, Teresa is receiving Holy Communion.

suggestion of that nonsense about my supposed sanctity. That allows me to live and go about without fear that the ridiculous tower of their imagination will come tumbling on top of me." Two years before she died, the pope recognized the reformed Carmelites as a separate religious order. Thirty five years after her death, when she had been beatified but not yet canonized, Teresa of Avila was proclaimed the patron of her country.

SAINT TERESA IS THE PATRON SAINT OF SPAIN, THOSE IN SPIRITUAL NEED, HEADACHES, AND LACEMAKERS.

MARTIN DE PORRES

1579–1639

MARTIN DE PORRES, born in Lima, Peru, was the natural son of a white Spanish nobleman and a free black woman. As a young man, Martin was apprenticed to a barber-surgeon, but he wanted to become a Dominican. He was not allowed to take the vows of a friar because his parents had not been married and because he was a mulatto (mixed race). Instead, he started working in a Dominican friary as a general helper. With typical humility, Martin did not resent this injustice.

"A man of great charity, who not only healed his brother religious when they were sick, but also helped in the larger duty of spreading God's Great Love of the world."

He cared for all living creatures no matter how humble, and ran a hospital for cats and dogs. The friars came to realize that Martin was a very able and holy man.

This painting of the black saint with his child assistant is found in Trujillo Cathedral in Peru.

SAINT MARTIN DE PORRES IS THE PATRON SAINT OF BARBERS AND PUBLIC HEALTH, AND AGAINST RACIAL INJUSTICE.

The distressed people who came to the friary were comforted by Martin. He was not afraid of catching the plague, and he became famous as a miracle-working healer. He was very concerned for street children and for people who suffered from racial prejudice.

In time, the brothers were looking to Martin for spiritual guidance. They were deeply ashamed of their earlier prejudice, and in 1610 they asked him to become a lay-brother. They helped Martin to set up a school for poor children and a hospital.

In the last year of Martin's life, the new Archbishop of Mexico asked him to come and work with him in Mexico. The archbishop made this suggestion because he did not think it was right that Martin was regarded as a living saint. Martin had agreed to leave Lima when he became ill and died of a fever. The whole city mourned his passing, but it was not until 1962 that Martin was canonized.

ROSE OF LIMA

1586-1617

ROSE grew up in Lima, the capital city of Peru. After her father lost money in a mining business, her family struggled to make ends meet, and Rose had to work at sewing and growing flowers. Her mother was anxious for her to get married, but Rose was determined to remain single and to dedicate her life to God. It was only when she was 20 that her mother allowed her to join the Dominicans as a Tertiary.

"Lord, increase my sufferings and with them increase thy love in my heart."

Tertiary, or third, religious orders were a way of enabling people to live like a monk or a nun without having to go to a monastery or convent. As a Tertiary, Rose lived alone in a summerhouse in her parents' garden. She put herself through a tough regime of fasting, praying for hours and doing without sleep. Some members of her family were shocked by Rose's harsh lifestyle, but other visitors—poor and sick people—were comforted by her. No one who met Rose doubted her kindness and sincerity.

SAINT ROSE OF LIMA IS THE PATRON SAINT OF THE AMERICAS, PERU, THE PHILIPPINES, LIMA, FLORISTS, AND GARDENERS.

Rose of Lima wears the black and white habit of a Dominican nun. The crown of roses is always associated with her.

After a long illness, which forced her to move back to her parents' house, Rose died. She was only 31. By then she was famous in Lima and beyond, and thousands of people mourned her as a saintly woman. In 1671, Rose of Lima was canonized, becoming the first saint of the Americas.

VINCENT DE PAUL

1581–1660

SAINT VINCENT DE PAUL IS THE PATRON SAINT OF CHARITABLE ORGANIZATIONS, HOSPITALS, PRISONERS, HORSES, AND SPIRITUAL WORK.

Vincent with members of the Sisters of Charity, who helped him with his charitable work.

VINCENT DE PAUL packed several lives into his 80 years. He was the son of a poor French farmer and became a priest when he was only 19. In 1605, while he was sailing from Marseilles, he was captured by pirates and sold as a slave in Tunisia. After two years, he managed to escape. Then he continued with his studies and went to Paris, where he became a court chaplain.

Vincent de Paul used his contacts with the French royal family and the nobility to reform and revitalize the Church. As a friend of the powerful Gondi family, he was able to improve the lot of convicts who had been sentenced to death. Even though he lived in Paris, he was eager to improve relations between country priests and their parishioners. From his priory at Saint-Lazare, he directed a vast network of new organizations which improved the training of priests and involved lay people in charitable work. He had a knack for finding the right people for the right job, and in 1633 he helped Louise de Marillac to found the Sisters of Charity.

"Monsieur Paul" became a legend in his own lifetime. It is said that he once tried to persuade the authorities to clap him in irons in place of a married convict. Today he is best known by the charitable organization that bears his name, the Society of Vincent de Paul, which was founded in 1833.

"We should spend as much time in thanking God for his benefits as we do in asking for them."

(*Right*) Antoine Ansiaux, a 19th-century painter, shows Vincent with the Sisters of Charity helping those dying from the plague.

LOUISE DE MARILLAC

1591–1660

Louise holding her rosary beads and wearing the habit of the Sisters of Charity.

In 1633 four young women moved into her Paris house and began to work as teachers and nurses among the city's poor. Louise drew up their first rule. Unlike traditional nuns, the Sisters of Charity were not based in a convent. Their convent was to be "the sickroom, their chapel the parish church, their cloister the streets of the city." They did not take religious vows until Vincent de Paul was persuaded to allow them to take vows for one year at a time.

The Sisters of Charity began to run the Hôtel-Dieu Hospital in Paris, as well as orphanages and schools. Louise de Marillac died in 1660, after reminding her Sisters that they should honor the poor and the sick "like Christ himself." The "butterfly" headdress of the Sisters of Charity, which was the everyday dress of Breton peasant women in the 17th century, was replaced by a more practical uniform in the 1960s. Although Louise de Marillac is not as well known as the war nurse Florence Nightingale, she deserves equal recognition as a pioneer of modern nursing.

LOUISE DE MARILLAC was a wealthy widow when she asked Vincent de Paul how she could help him with his social work. He asked her to organize and train the first Sisters of Charity because Louise was as practical as she was idealistic. She had nursed her invalid husband, and unlike other wealthy widows who helped Vincent de Paul, she welcomed hard work.

"Love the poor and honor them as you would honor Christ."

ELIZABETH SETON

1774–1821

Elizabeth Seton was the first native-born American to be canonized. When Elizabeth was 19, she married a merchant named William Magee Seton. They had five children, but Elizabeth still found time for charitable work. In 1797 she formed the Society for the Relief of Poor Widows with Small Children.

Five years later, William's business began to fail, and then he became seriously ill. In the hope that he would get better, Elizabeth took him to Italy, but he died in Pisa in 1803. For five months Elizabeth remained in Italy, where she was looked after by her friends, the Filicchi family. The Filicchis were devout Catholics, and Elizabeth was so impressed by them that two years later in New York she was baptized as a Catholic.

In 1808 she was asked to open a Catholic school for girls in Baltimore. Soon afterward she pronounced her first vows and received the title of Mother. In 1809 she and her first followers began community life in Emmitsburg, Maryland, which has been the headquarters of the American Sisters of Charity ever since.

"Lord God, You blessed Saint Elizabeth Ann Seton with gifts of grace as wife, mother, educator, and foundress, so that she might spend her life in service to Your people."

Elizabeth Seton painted as the foundress of the American Sisters of Charity, holding rosary beads.

The American Sisters worked as teachers and nurses. Under Mother Seton's direction, they started new schools, clinics, and orphanages. When she died in 1821, there were 20 communities of the Sisters of Charity and orphanages in Philadelphia and New York.

MODERN SAINTS

The stories of the saints reflect the history of Christianity. There is a saint for every time, including our own, but while they were living, the saints never thought of themselves as such. In 1933, a shy French woman named Marie-Bernarde Soubirous was canonized. She is better known to us as Saint Bernadette. Bernadette was the eldest child of a poor miller. She was small for her age and suffered dreadfully from asthma. In 1858, when she was fourteen, she had a series of visions of the Blessed Virgin Mary, who appeared to her at Lourdes in a shallow cave in the banks of the River Gave. "The Lady" asked Bernadette to build a church there and to drink water from a nearby spring. Although Bernadette's extraordinary experience led to the foundation of a great healing shrine, she resisted attempts to turn her into a celebrity. She was not present at the consecration of the Lourdes Basilica in 1876 and spent her adult life quietly as an unassuming nun.

The Italian saint, John (Giovanni) Bosco (1815-1888), was from a similarly humble background. His father died when he was two, leaving his mother to bring up three boys in extreme poverty. While he was growing up, John liked to hang around circus camps, and he learned how to juggle and walk a tight-rope. After a dream in which he saw himself turning beasts into lambs, he decided to become a priest. While he was a student priest in Turin, he started working in the slums. He was very popular because he did not treat slum kids like juvenile delinquents. With his mother's help, he set up a hostel, where boys could live and train as tailors and shoemakers. These activities were so successful that he founded an order, named after Saint Francis de Sales. By the time

Saint Bernadette as a young girl before she joined the Sisters of Notre-Dame of Nevers.

The grotto, as it is today, where Mary appeared to Bernadette in Lourdes, France.

A painting of Father John Bosco with some of the young boys that he helped shown in the background.

of his death, 764 Salesian brothers were working in cities all over the world.

Although it is increasingly hard to define saintliness in traditional ways, the lengthy and painstaking business of canonization continues. The first step to sainthood is beatification, declaring a person to be "Blessed." In March 1998, while he was visiting Nigeria, Pope John Paul II beatified Father Cyprian Michael Tansi. The Blessed Father Tansi was born in 1903 in a small African village. His father died when he was a boy, but his uncle arranged for him to attend a Christian school. In 1922 his elderly mother was forced to drink a deadly poison by the local voodoo priest, and this tragedy determined Tansi to spread

Father Cyprian Michael Tansi

Christianity among his people. In 1937 he was ordained, and he spent the following years studying, teaching, and building churches, schools, and clinics. His energy and the warmth of his personality made him a cult figure, but he didn't like to be treated as anyone special. In 1950 his order, the Cistercians, allowed him to retire as a contemplative monk. So it was that the African priest spent his last years in an enclosed monastery in Leicestershire in Britain. In 1986 his remains were exhumed from the abbey's cemetery and flown back to Nigeria. Five hundred thousand people attended the ceremony of beatification, the first time that such a ceremony had been conducted outside the Vatican.

GLOSSARY

Abbot
The leader, or superior, of a community of monks living in an abbey or monastery.

Anchorite
A monk or hermit who lives alone.

Assumption
Mary, the Mother of God, is believed to have been taken, or assumed, in the flesh straight to Heaven because she was free from sin and immediately deserving of eternal life.

Baptism
The ceremony of being dipped in or sprinkled with water, which has been the rite of entry to the Christian faith since the time of John the Baptist.

Barbarians
The name given by the ancient Greeks, and then the Romans, to peoples who lived outside their own civilization.

Bohemia
A kingdom in central Europe that is now part of the Czech Republic. Prague is in Bohemia.

Byzantium
The Greek city which, early in the fourth century, was rebuilt by the Emperor Constantine. As Constantinople it became the capital of the Eastern Roman Empire. Since its conquest by the Ottoman ruler Mehmed II in 1453, it has been known as Istanbul.

Canonization
The process by which the Catholic Church declares a dead holy person is a saint worthy of veneration by Christians. Before being canonized, the saint must have performed verifiable miracles.

Chastity
Monks and nuns took vows of chastity, meaning that they would not have sex and would remain celibate, or unmarried.

Commandments
The Ten Commandments are the laws or rules of God which, according to the Bible, were given to Moses in the form of stone tablets while he was on Mount Sinai.

Conversion
The process by which a person changes, or converts, from one religion or set of beliefs to another.

Council of Trent
Between 1545 and 1563 a council of leading churchmen met at Trent (now in northern Italy). They were hoping to reform the Catholic Church, so that Protestants could rejoin it. This never happened, but Pope Pius V put many of their decisions into effect. As a result, Catholic worship throughout the world was standardized. This is called the Counter-Reformation.

Crosier
The traditional staff of a bishop, shaped like a shepherd's crook to symbolize his role as a shepherd of Christians.

Crusade
Wars organized by European popes and princes to recapture the holy lands of the Middle East from Islam.

Doctrine
The most important Christian beliefs as they have been organized and defined by the Catholic Church.

Druids
The priests and judges of ancient Celtic societies, such as pre-Christian Ireland, who were in charge of religious ceremonies.

Emblem
A sign or symbol that stands for something different from itself. The emblems by which saints are identified usually refer to an episode of their lives or an aspect of their characters. For example, the legendary Saint Barbara is represented by a tower because she was said to have been imprisoned in one by her father.

Evangelists
Matthew, Mark, Luke, and John, the authors of the four gospels are known as the Evangelists, which means "bringers of good news."

Excommunicate
To be excommunicated is to be expelled from the Church and deprived of the sacraments, such as holy communion or confession.

Exile
To be exiled is to be sent far away from your home country. In the past, rulers often dealt with troublemakers by exiling them.

Faith
Belief, or trust, in the teachings of a religion.

Gentile
A non-Jewish person.

Gospels
The first four books of the New Testament, the part of the Bible that records the life and teachings of Jesus.

Heretic
A person who believes or teaches ideas about Christianity that are contrary to the doctrine of the Catholic Church.

Holy Spirit
Also known as the Holy Ghost, or the Paraclete, the third aspect of the Christian Trinity.

Idol
A statue or an image of a non-Christian god.

Indulgence
A kind of pardon for sin that in medieval times could be gained through acts or works of charity, such as a pilgrimage to a shrine or a contribution to the building of a church. The way in which indulgences were sold by church officials was one of Martin Luther's complaints about the Catholic Church.

Interdict
A sentence by a pope forbidding a person, church, or region to practice the rites of the Catholic Church. The interdict was often in response to wrongdoing by the local ruler. Usually, an exception was made for the baptism of babies and the absolution of the dying.

Koran
The holy book of Islam, which contains Allah's teachings as revealed to the Prophet Muhammad.

Liturgy
The words used for the celebration of Christian rites.

Magnificat
The song of joy and thanksgiving that, according to the Gospel of Saint Luke, Mary spoke when she found out that she was to become the mother of God.

Meditation
The act of thinking deeply on a spiritual theme.

Messiah
From Hebrew words for "Anointed One," meaning the great leader whose coming was prophesied in the Old Testament. Christians believe that Jesus is this promised Messiah, or "Christ."

Miter
The traditional high, pointed headdress of Christian bishops.

New Testament
The part of the Christian Bible that includes the gospels written by Matthew, Mark, Luke, and John, as well as the Acts of the Apostles and Saint Paul's letters.

Old Testament
The ancient Hebrew books of the Bible, including the Psalms, which are holy to both Jews and Christians.

Ordain
A person is ordained, or officially admitted to holy orders, so that he or she can act as a minister or a priest.

Pacifist
Someone who believes that violence is never justified. Instead of joining a war against injustice, a pacifist might resort to peaceful protest or passive resistance.

Pagan
From the Latin word for a country person, often used by pioneering Christians to describe Europeans who had not encountered the new religion.

Parable
A story or fable that explains or gives example of Christian behavior. The Good Samaritan and the Prodigal Son are characters from two of the best-known parables in the New Testament.

Passover
The Jewish spring festival that celebrates the freeing of the Israelites from slavery in Egypt. It happens around the same time as Easter.

Patron Saint
Traditionally, particular saints have been adopted by particular groups as their special protector, or "patron."

Penance
Ways in which people try to show how sorry they are for wrongdoing and make amends, often imposed by a priest.

Pentecost
A Christian festival commemorating the descent of the Holy Spirit to the Apostles. It occurs 50 days after Easter, originally on the same day as the Jewish holiday of Shavuot.

Persecution
Throughout history, individuals and whole communities have been persecuted, that is, they have suffered ill-treatment and even death because of their beliefs.

Pilgrims
Travelers to a holy place or shrine.

Plainsong
A style of medieval church music, which is also called Plainchant or Gregorian Chant.

Prophet
A great religious leader whose teachings are believed to have been inspired by God.

Psalm
The songs or hymns of the Bible's Book of Psalms.

Quill
A pen made from a sharpened feather dipped in ink. Goose feathers make the best quills.

Rabbi
A teacher or leader of a Jewish community.

Relic
Part of the bodily remains of a saint.

Resurrection
The third day after the Crucifixion, when Jesus rose from the dead.

Rhetoric
The art of speaking to influence, persuade, or please, often used by preachers, politicians, and lawyers.

Rite
A religious ceremony.

Sin
Wrongdoing, especially against the Ten Commandments, that offends God.

Spirit
Another word for the "soul," the part of a human being responsible for thinking and knowing right and wrong. Often considered immortal.

Theology
From the Greek for "science of God," the study of divinity.

Transfiguration
When Jesus talked with the prophets Elias and Moses on the mountain, he was "transfigured," made radiant, by a brilliant divine light. The apostles Peter, James, and John were with him.

Veneration
Canonized saints are deemed worthy of reverence, which means that they can be venerated, that is, prayed to and regarded as holy.

INDEX

CALENDAR OF SAINTS

JANUARY

1 **Blessed Virgin Mary** (see pages 10–11); Odilo; Joseph Tomasi
2 **Basil the Great** (see page 35) and Gregory of Nazianzus
3 Fulgentius; Geneviève
4 **Elizabeth Seton** (see page 75)
5 John Nepomucene Neumann; Simeon the Stylite
6 Peter of Canterbury
7 Canute Lavard; Lucian of Antioch
8 Gudula; Pega; Lucian of Beauvais; Severinus of Noricum
9 Adrian of Canterbury; Philip of Moscow
10 Peter Orseolo
11 Paulinus of Aquileia; Theodosius the Cenobiarch
12 Benedict (or Benet) Biscop; Tatiana
13 Hilary of Poitiers; Antony Pucci
14 **Macrina the Elder** (see page 35)
15 Ita; Macarius the Elder; Paul the Hermit
16 Berard and his companions; Fursey; Honoratus of Arles
17 **Antony of Egypt** (see pages 30–31); Sulpice
18 Margaret of Hungary; Prisca
19 Canute IV; Henry of Uppsala; Wulfstan
20 Euthymius the Great; Fabian and Sebastian
21 **Agnes** (see page 27); Meinrad
22 Anastasius the Persian; Vincent of Saragossa; Vincent Pallotti
23 Ildefonsus; John the Almsgiver
24 Francis de Sales
25 Juventinus and Maximinus; Conversion of **Paul** (see pages 16–17)
26 Alberic; Eystein; Paula; Timothy and Titus
27 Angela of Brescia
28 Peter Nolasco; **Thomas Aquinas** (see pages 7 and 58–59)
29 Gildas the Wise; Sulpicius
30 Bathild; Martina
31 Cyrus and John; **John Bosco** (see pages 76–77); Marcella

FEBRUARY

1 Brigid of Ireland
2 Joan de Lestonnac
3 Anskar; Blaise; Lawrence of Canterbury; Werburgh
4 Andrew Corsini; Joan of France; Phileas
5 Agatha
6 Amand of Maastricht; Dorothy
7 Richard; Theodore the General
8 Cuthman; Jerome Emiliani; John of Matha
9 Apollonia; Nicephorus of Antioch; Teilo

10 **Scholastica** (see page 40)
11 Benedict of Aniane
12 Julian the Hospitaller; Marina
13 Catherine dei Ricci
14 **Cyril and Methodius** (see page 44); Maro; Valentine
15 Sigfrid
16 Elias and his companions
17 Finan; Fintan of Clonenagh; Seven Servite Founders
18 Colman of Lindisfarne; Flavian of Constantinople
19 Mesrop
20 Shahdost; Ulric of Haselbury
21 Peter Damian
22 Margaret of Cortona
23 Mildburga; Polycarp; Willigis
24 Montanus and Lucius
25 Ethelbert of Kent; Walburga
26 Porphyry of Gaza
27 Gabriel Possenti; Leander
28 Oswald of Worcester

MARCH

1 David (or Dewi)
2 Chad
3 Aelred; Cunegund; Marinus of Caesarea; Winaloe
4 Casimir
5 Ciaran of Saighir; Phocas of Antioch; Piran
6 Chrodegang; Colette; Cyneburga
7 **Perpetua and Felicity** (see page 27)
8 Felix of Dunwich; John of God; Julian of Toledo
9 Frances of Rome; Gregory of Nyssa; Catherine of Bologna
10 John Ogilvie
11 Eulogius of Córdova; Sophronius
12 Maximilian; Simeon the New Theologian
13 Euphrasia; Gerald of Mayo
14 Matilda
15 Clement Hofbauer; **Louise de Marillac** (see page 74)
16 Heribert of Cologne; Julian of Antioch; Paul the Simple
17 Gertrude of Nivelles; Joseph of Arimathaea; **Patrick** (see page 38)
18 Cyril of Jerusalem; Edward the Martyr
19 **Joseph** (see pages 10–11)
20 Cuthbert; Herbert of Derwentwater
21 Enda; Nicholas von Flue
22 Zachary
23 Gwinear; Turibius of Mogrovejo
24 Catherine of Vadstena
25 Alfwold; Dismas
26 Braulio; Ludger; William of Norwich
27 John the Egyptian; Rupert of Salzburg
28 Alkelda of Middleham
29 Berthold; Jonah and Berikjesu;

Mark of Arethusa
30 John Climacus; Osburga

APRIL

1 Hugh of Grenoble
2 Francis of Paola; Mary the Egyptian
3 Pancras of Taormina; Richard of Chichester
4 Benedict the Black; Isidore
5 Vincent Ferrer
6 William of Aebelholt
7 John Baptist de La Salle; Nilus of Sora
8 Perpetuus
9 Waudru
10 Fulbert of Chartres
11 Gemma Galgani; **Stanislaus of Cracow** (see page 46)
12 Sabas the Goth; Zeno of Verona
13 Carpus and Papylus; Martin I
14 Tiburtius
15 Paternus of Wales
16 Benedict Labre; **Bernadette** (see page 76); Magnus of Orkney
17 Donnan; Robert of Chaise-Dieu; Stephen Harding
18 Laserian, Apollonius
19 Alphege; Expeditus; Leo IX
20 Agnes of Montepulciano
21 Anselm; Beuno; Simeon Barsabba'e
22 Conrad of Parzham; Pherbutha; Theodore of Sykeon
23 Adalbert of Prague; George
24 Euphrasia Pelletier; Ivo; Mellitus
25 **Mark** (see pages 22–23); William of Monte Vergine
26 Cletus; Stephen of Perm
27 Maughold; Zita
28 Louis Grignion; Paul of the Cross; Peter Chanel
29 **Catherine of Siena** (see page 57); Hugh of Cluny; Robert of Molesme
30 Joseph Cottonlengo; Marian and James; Pius V

MAY

1 Brieuc; **Joseph** (see pages 10–11)
2 Athanasius
3 Philip and James the Less; Theodosius of the Caves
4 Gothard; Pelagia of Tarsus
5 Hilary of Arles; Jutta
6 Marian and James
7 John of Beverley; Lindhard
8 Peter of Tarentaise; Victor
9 Pachomius
10 Antonino; John of Avila
11 Asaph; Comgall; Francis di Girolamo; Mayeul
12 Epiphanius of Salamis; Ignatius of Laconi; Pancras
13 Andrew Fournet; Euthymius the Enlightener

14 Mary Mazzarello; Matthias; Michael Garicoïts
15 Dympna; Hallvard
16 Brendan the Voyager; Simon Stock
17 Paschal Baylon
18 Eric; Felix of Cantalice
19 Celestine V; Dunstan; Yves
20 Bernardine of Siena; Ethelbert of East Anglia
21 Godric
22 Rita of Cascia
23 Desiderius; Ivo of Chartres; William of Rochester
24 David of Scotland; Simeon Stylite the Younger
25 Gregory VII; The Three Marys
26 Mariana of Quito; Philip Neri
27 **The Venerable Bede** (see page 42); Augustine of Canterbury; Julius of Durostorum
28 Bernard of Montjoux; Germanus of Paris
29 Bona of Pisa
30 Ferdinand III of Castille; **Joan of Arc** (see pages 62–63)
31 Petronilla

JUNE

1 Justin; Pamphilus
2 Erasmus (or Elmo); Marcellinus and Peter
3 Clotilda; Kevin
4 Francis Caracciolo; Petroc
5 **Boniface** (see page 43)
6 Jarlath of Tuam; Norbert
7 Meriadoc; Robert of Newminster
8 Melania the Elder; William of York
9 **Columba** (or Columcille) (see page 39); Pelagia of Antioch
10 Ithamar
11 Barnabas
12 Eskil; John of Sahagun; Leo III
13 **Antony of Padua** (see page 4)
14 Methodius of Constantinople
15 Edburga of Winchester; Germaine of Pibrac; Vitus
16 Cyricus and Julitta; John Regis; Lutgard; Tikhon of Amathus
17 Botolph (or Botulf); Harvey
18 Elizabeth of Schönau; Mark and Marcellian
19 Gervase and Protase; Juliana Falconieri
20 Adalbert of Magdeburg
21 Aloysius; Méen
22 Alban; John Fisher; **Thomas More** (see page 49); Nicetas of Remesiana
23 Etheldreda (or Audrey); Joseph Cafasso
24 **John the Baptist** (birth) (see pages 12–13)
25 Febronia; Prosper of Reggio
26 Anthelm; **John** (see pages 20–21) and **Paul** (see pages 8 and 16–17)